# An Enemy
# More Deadly Than Death

Skeelie sat up, fuzzy with sleep, the night dreams hardly separated from the gray shadows of the room, and began to rummage in her pack for food. A small sound stopped her. The door latch was lifting.

She snatched up her bow, as the door pushed in noiselessly, her heart pounding, sleep cast aside. What was that smell? Like something dead.

Then she saw the hand feeling in through the crack of the door. A thin, white hand. The door pushed in in one quick movement, and a dark figure stood looking at her, a faceless silhouette. It stood watching her. And Skeelie knew it had come here to die, and it meant to take her body in place of its own dying one . . .

*Other Avon Books*
*in* The Children of Ynell Series *by*
**Shirley Rousseau Murphy**


THE CASTLE OF HAPE
THE RING OF FIRE
THE WOLF BELL


*Coming Soon*


THE JOINING OF THE STONE

---

# CAVES OF FIRE AND ICE

SHIRLEY ROUSSEAU
MURPHY

AN AVON FLARE BOOK

AVON BOOKS
A division of
The Hearst Corporation
959 Eighth Avenue
New York, New York 10019

The Atheneum Books edition contains the following Library of Congress
Cataloging in Publication Data:

Murphy, Shirley Rousseau.
Caves of fire and ice.

SUMMARY: Followed by faithful Skeelie and the wolves,
Ramad aides heroes of many ages on the planet Ere,
but seems forever separated from Telien
as she fulfills a fate of her own.
[1. Fantasy] I. Title.
PZ7.M956Car        [Fic]        80-12887

First Flare Printing, March, 1982

# Contents

MAP of ERE

# Part One

*The Lake of Fire*

*The battle of the Castle of Hape was ended, the Hape defeated and the castle burned to ashes and flame-blackened stone. Ramad of Carriol rode away from that victory surrounded by the wolves who had fought so fiercely beside him. He stood that night high on a cliff beside his supper fire as, before him, come out of Time itself, appeared the white-haired time-wanderer who called himself Anchorstar. But even as they spoke, Time warped again; and Ramad beheld the face of his true love, the face of Telien. He held her but an instant before they were whirled away on Time's tide, flung far, one from the other, into Time's ever-surging reaches. Lovers destined to wander forever apart upon Time's dark unpredictable shores? Who could say? Perhaps no Seer could predict such a thing.*

*Many mourned Ramad, gone from his own time. And never would he return there. Skeelie of Carriol mourned him, the brother of her spirit, the lover she wanted but could not have, mourned him for three long days before she armed herself to follow Ramad through the barrier of Time. Determined to follow him, to find a way across that dark, capricious threshold.*

*Alone, she went into the high caves of Owdneet where lay buried secrets that might guide her across Time's currents, and she carried the silver sword Ram had forged for her. Though he loved another, she would follow him; she could do nothing less. The misery without him was too great.*

From *The Mystery of Ramad*, Book of Carriol. Signed Meren Hoppa. Written in Carriol some time after her escape from the caves of Kubal.

# Chapter One

SHE HAD BEEN seven days in the caves, wandering in darkness. There was light enough in the great central grotto, daylight, then the light from Ere's moons on most nights. But away from the grotto, deeper in the mountain, in the small caves and tunnels where she searched, no light came, and her oil lamp hardly cut the darkness. The silence in the low, tight tunnels was absolute and cold. She had squinted over stone tablets carved with the history of Ere, crouched frowning in the dim light to unroll and study parchments stacked one atop the next, row on row of them in stone niches in the cave walls, but had found as yet no trace of the runes for which she searched. Patiently she rolled each one up again, more discouraged each time.

Her food was nearly gone. She was sick of dried mountain meat, dry mawzee cakes, the metallic tasting cave water. And the lamp oil was running low. Soon she would have to leave the caves to hunt, or there would be no fat to render into oil. She could not search for anything in darkness. But hunting would take precious time, for all the rising peaks had been black and withered when she came up the mountain seven days before. There would be little game. In the caves, the air still smelled of smoke. She fingered her bow, ran an exploring finger over the silver hilt of her sword and remembered painfully when Ram had forged it. They had been children then, come recently out of Burgdeeth. She had carried it all these years, fought and killed with it, had fought the Herebian raiders these last months, with the sword so much a part of her she hardly remembered it had been made by Ram's hand. Now she remembered, sharply and painfully, as Ram's face filled her thoughts, his dark eyes intent and serious, a thatch of his red hair falling across his forehead, the line of his long, lean face caught in firelight as she had last seen him in painful vision, before he was swept into Time.

She picked up the lantern, sighing, and turned deeper into the mountain.

He did not love her, could never love her. Because of Telien. If she found him with Telien in some idyl far in Time, she could only turn away again to lose herself in Time unending, in desolation unending. And yet she must follow him, she could do nothing else.

Who knew where Time had swept him, or to what purpose? Truly to follow Telien? Or had some evil reached to touch Ram, to open Time to him?

She searched for long hours, hardly pausing to eat. She had all but lost her sense of time. Night was no different than day. She slept little, wrapped in her cloak for an hour or so, always cold. Woke and went on until she grew exhausted or very discouraged, slept again. There was enough lamp oil for perhaps four more fillings.

Then came the moment when she woke from a light sleep suddenly, startled, struck her flint hastily to the lamp. What had awakened her? There was a difference in the cave, she felt a new sense, a sense of something pulling at her.

Confused and yawning, trying to collect her wits, she rose, jumbled her scattered belongings into her pack, and began to make her way toward that beckoning hope, prodding her anew. Her dark hair, bundled into an untidy bun, had slipped down to her shoulder. Her bow and quiver hung crooked across her pack. Her leather tunic was wrinkled, her wrists protruding from her sleeves. Her dark eyes were intent and haunted. What had reached out so suddenly to wake her, to pull at her? She followed with growing urgency. Had her need to search out the secrets of Time at last awakened some magic deep within the mountain? But why? She had found no key, yet, to unlocking those secrets. Nor did she carry one of the starfires, such as Anchorstar had given to Ram, to quicken the magic of Time. What called to her, then, from deep within the mountain?

And if she found a way into Time's reaches, where would that way lead her? To Ram, or a million years from Ram? Once she crossed Time's barrier, would she have the skills to find Ram? Uncountable centuries swept away to a future unborn and backward to incredible violence and turmoil. How *could* one enter Time, enter a future unborn? Yet it had happened to Skeelie and Ram when they were children—Time rocking asunder, future and past coming together. That moment had changed the very history of Ere, that moment on Tala-charen when the runestone of Eresu split, when men and women came out of Time to receive the shards of that shattered jade.

She knew she should turn back to hunt and replenish the lamp oil, but could not deny the power that drew her. She followed the beckoning sense down a dark, narrowing tunnel, pushing always deeper inside the mountain. She had been so tired, but now she moved quickly, the chill gone, hunger unheeded. She remembered the quick vision she had had ten days before of Ram standing beside his supper fire, then suddenly Telien with him, her pale hair caught in moonlight as she reached out of Time itself to hold Ram. Then the sense of the night twisting in on itself, Ram swept out of Telien's arms shouting her name over and over, uselessly. Ram alone, and the trees only saplings once more—and then the hill empty as Ram himself was swept away in Time's invisible river.

The tunnel became so low she had to walk bent over, her hair catching in the stone of the roof, very aware suddenly of the weight of the mountain above her, tons of stone above her. She turned the lamp lower to save oil, knew she must save two fillings to return to the main grotto or be trapped in darkness. The press of stone against her shoulders made her want to strike out, want to drive the mountain back. She controlled herself with effort, pulled urgently forward by something insistent, something compelling. Something evil? Was that which beckoned to her evil?

At last the tunnel ended, and she stood in a cave that

seemed not bounded by walls, seemed to warp and to hint of distant, terrifying reaches. Her guttering light caught at uncertain shadows and at dark so thick that light could not penetrate it. Nothing was clear, but the cave seemed to extend far beyond any area the mountain could possibly contain. A terror of infinite space yawned beyond her vision, and suddenly she could not bring herself to go forward, was terrified of the very thing she sought, terrified of falling into Time, of being lost in Time. All her determination disappeared, and the fear she had kept at bay so long overwhelmed her. She wanted to turn back, wanted to run blindly. She stood with clenched fists, trying to control herself. You've come this far, Skeelie. You can't turn back. You can't run away now. She was caught between her sudden horror of the unknown and her need to become a part of that dark emptiness in Time where Ram was. She moved on at last, shivering.

Soon she could make out something painted on the walls. She held the lamp up. Scenes of farms and villages, of battles, scenes shifting between shadows, then changing as she moved on. Who had painted such images so deep in the caves? Her lamp sputtered and grew dim.

Then the scenes came clearer and seemed larger suddenly, crowding toward her between the chasms of darkness. Scenes of war and violence leaped out at her; men opened their mouths in silent screams as swords flashed. She heard the din of war faintly, then it rose in volume until it deafened her. She smelled blood and death. Had she moved into Time suddenly? Clouds raced across dark skies. All was movement and shouting, a dozen places in a dozen times. She was caught like a fly at the center, suddenly mad with desire to thrust herself into those scenes. She searched for Ram's face among infinite battles, searched for a flash of his red hair. Once she reached out her naked hand toward a battle, then snatched it back and pressed it to her mouth to stifle the cry that rose: for the shadows had changed to form themselves into a twisting tree. The battles faded. The tree filled the cave, huge and pulsing with life. It pushed gnarled branches against the cave walls, forcing up, bending against the dirt roof. Its bark was rough and dark, its roots humped like twisted, naked legs across the cave floor. Its trunk was wrinkled into seams and angles that formed the face of an old, old man. His eyes watched her from some terrible depth. Eyes cold and knowing, eyes like windows into Time. His voice was like the rasp of winter wind.

*I watched you come. I watched you search. I know what you seek here. You will find it, young woman. You will move through Time unending, and you will suffer for that. Time cares nothing for your suffering. And you care nothing for reason if you plunge into Time's reaches.*

"I do what I must. I can do nothing else." She held her shaking hands still with effort. "Who are you? What—sort of creature are you?"

*I am Cadach. I have dwealt in this tree since my death.* He watched her fear of him, in spite of her bold stance. *My soul dwells here. It cannot move on, nor yet can it die utterly. Traitor in my life, traitor to Ere, my soul can never move on, can never be born anew. I can only wait. My children wander Time endlessly. My children atone for me.* His sense of agony filled Skeelie. *My children know not that I exist here. They know not why they are driven. They know only that their need is to reach out, to hold a light to the darkness that comes again and again upon Ere. For they, each one, carry within the higher spirit that I would have become. That I denied with my evil. They carry that spirit within them, which I will never carry. My five white-haired children.*

His voice went silent and his face seemed carven once more, then collapsed as it began to recede back into the bark. Skeelie stood staring, shaken, wanting stupidly to cry out for him not to leave her. His eyes, dull and lifeless now, disappeared last. She backed away from the trunk. His fading voice breathed out once more, hollow now, hardly a whisper. *Follow you through the maze of this cave as your mind bids you, Seer.* She strained to hear. *Follow you the path of the starfires. Find the Cutter of Stones who made them, for he will give you strength. Follow to the source of Ramad's beginnings, touch the place of his childhood and his strength. And know you that Ramad must search through Time for more than his lost love, know you that he must search for the lost shards of the runestone of Eresu if he be true to himself.* She could hardly make out his words, leaned closer to the hoary bark; and one question burned in her.

"How do I know I *can* move into Time? I do not carry starfires. I do not touch Time's secrets, nor have I found a rune with its secrets."

*You are one of the few born outside the progression of souls. You. Ramad. Telien. Those so born can deal with Time sufficiently.*

"I do not understand."

But he was gone. The ancient tree slept, retreating into a million years of repose whence its core had risen. Skeelie moved past it into the darker shadows, wondering, trying to make sense of his words. How could the old man know of Ram, of the starfires? Surely he was a Seer. A Seer trapped, his immortal soul taken. A Seer of evil? A traitor as had been BroogArl, and HarThass before him? A traitor trapped so, never to be born again? She shivered. And his white-haired children . . .

Could Anchorstar be one of Cadach's children? Anchorstar—*my white-haired children.* . . . Anchorstar had carried the starfires, had given one to Telien, had given three to Ram. *Follow you the path of the starfires . . .*

Her stomach was knotted. Her hand clutched her sword hilt. Her mind raced eagerly ahead between the dark reaches, seeking now with awe, pushing toward those other worlds that had begun again to shine around her, toward the cries of men in battle, listening for Ram's voice. Voids and piercing space threatened to swallow her. She left each scene behind her for she could not find Ram. She sought deeper and deeper into the mountain.

Then she came suddenly to a pillar carved with runes that made her catch her breath, for three words shone out at her. Words so familiar, so very painful: *Eternal. Will sing.* Those words had been carved on the splinter of the runestone that Ram had brought with him out of Talacharen, the splinter that now lay at the bottom of the sea, lost when the Hape had nearly killed Ram. They had never known the whole rune that appeared on the complete, unbroken stone. Ram had not had time to read it in that instant before it shattered. But these three words were part of it, and they blazed at her like fire from the pillar.

> *Eternal quest to those with power.*
> *Some seek dark; they mortal end.*
> *Some hold joy; they know eternal life,*
> *Through them all powers will sing.*

Were these words the whole rune that was carved into the runestone? Who had carved it here in this buried place? She reached out, shaking, to touch the carved pillar. What linking did this tablet have to the runestone? What linking to Ram, in whose hands the stone had shattered? She turned suddenly, feeling watched, feeling another presence.

Or was it only the old man, still watching her? Her nerves were strung tight. Imagining things. Imagining for a moment a sense of dark evil drawing in around her; and then gone. She returned to puzzling over the carved tablet. The lantern was burning low, would soon need refilling. Were the words on the tablet the key for which she searched, the key into Time? She stood repeating the words, then turned away at last confused and dizzy, and felt space wheeling around her and sudden heat searing her. Then winds came, and scenes overlapped in wild succession. She felt she could not breathe. She saw children running in terror before a river of fire, saw volcanoes spewing out against the sky. She searched wildly for a glimpse of Ram as a hundred scenes overwhelmed her. She knew she must move, must launch herself into this melee if she were to hurdle Time's barrier—but into which scene? She dared not fling herself a thousand years from Ram, yet how could she know? She searched frantically, could not see his face, was stifled by fear, by indecision. Her lantern sputtered, the flame died. But the scenes were dimly lit, taunting her, terrifying her. She dropped the lantern, heard the precious glass shatter. She wheeled around in impotent panic—and felt something brush her arm, solid and huge; leaped back in terror, sword drawn.

The flashing scenes were gone. Dim light shone above her from a star-struck sky. A black cliff rose beside her. She touched it again. The cliff of a mountain. She let out a long breath. She was no longer in the cave, had been swept without volition across the abyss. She was ashamed now of her fear and confusion. Looking up at the sky, at the stars, she felt their vast distance. A cold wind touched her face. The caves were gone, perhaps centuries gone. She had come at last into the unfathomable, where she could search for Ram.

Then she saw the fire.

It was some distance away, down to her left, a very small fire, like a campfire. Her heart was beating wild and quick with the knowledge that she had come through the impossible barrier. That campfire might mean anything: people or creatures beyond her comprehension.

The fire flickered, then was lost for a moment as something dark moved across it. Surely it was a campfire. The sharp tang of painon-wood smoke made her press her finger to her nose to keep from sneezing. The smell of searing meat brought water to her mouth. She was wild with hunger suddenly, like an animal. She stood staring down at the bright, small glow, trying in vain to make out figures or a shelter. Surely someone must be sitting huddled in shadow waiting for supper to cook. When a sharp, high noise cut the night, she startled terribly, swallowed, her hand tight on her drawn sword in quick mindless reflex.

But it had only been a goat, the high shrill bleat of a doe goat. The fire blazed bright as if its builder had laid on more wood. The meat smelled wonderful. She could see no one. She stood quietly, but her pulse still pounded wildly with the realization that she had at last left her own time. Suddenly a voice spoke. She spun and stared at the man before her, her sword pricking his chest.

"Good even'," he repeated.

How had he come so silently, slipping up on her? Her muscles were tense and ready to thrust, her blood surging with warlike reflex. Then she felt embarrassment, for he was only a small, elderly herder staring up at her, gentle of face, surprised by her quick, violent action. His voice was soft and even now, as if he spoke to a nervy beast.

"Sheath your sword, lad." He stepped back away from the tip of her blade. "Sheath it, I've no quarrel with you, nor mean you harm." He watched her lower her blade a trifle. "Hungry? Are ye hungry? Come on to the fire, then, lad. Don't be standing here staring, riling my goats all to thunder. Come down to the fire and settle. Who be ye, lad, coming out of the night so?"

# Chapter Two

THE HERDER TURNED his back on her, plainly expecting her
to follow as he made his way back toward the fire. He must
be simple, turning his back on a sword. Or could this man
be a Seer, know she meant no harm? She sought into his
mind warily. But no, only a simple man. Trusting her. He
led her to the fire, stooped to turn the roasting meat. Her
sword swung against a boulder, ringing sharply, and a buck,
startled, snorted. The animal stood just beyond the fire, a
big Cherban buck with horns as long as her sword and nearly
as sharp. Maybe this herder had more protection than she
had guessed. The man had turned, was surveying her with
surprise, now that he could see her clearly in the firelight.
"Why it ain't a lad at all!" He took in her knotted dark hair,
the curve of her breast beneath her tunic, her thin-boned
face. "A lady—in fighting leathers!" He studied her with
interest. "Old, scarred leathers, and stained with blood,
looks like." He reached to touch her sword, took it from
her in a gesture innocent and bold.

She, always so quick and careful, let him take it with
quiet amusement. He held it close to the flame where he
could make out the intricate carving of birds and leaves with
which the handle was fashioned, the clean, sharp blade.
Then he raised his eyes to her. "A fine sword, lady. Fine.
It was made with great skill. And with love."

His words brought unexpected pain. She looked away
from him, felt gone of strength, wanting to weep for no
reason. Made with love. Brotherly love, maybe. No more.
She straightened her shoulders and stared at him defiantly,
reached out for her sword. "How would you know if it was
made with love? That is skill you see. Only skill in the
casting of the silver."

"All skill, lady, is a matter of love. Have you not learned

22

that? I hope you know more about the use of the sword than you do about a man's mind."

"I know about its use. And I know more about men's minds than—" She stopped, had almost given herself away in anger. Stupid girl. Shout it out. Tell him you know all about men's minds, can see into men's minds, tell him you're a Seer! And who knows what they do to Seers in this time. Kill them? Behead them? Better collect yourself, Skeelie, find out where you are—and when—and stop acting like an injured river cat.

"Ain't never seen a lady got up so in fighting leathers."

She wanted to say, *Where I come from it's common enough.* She wanted to say, *What year is this that women don't fight beside their men?* But even in her own time, the women of the coastal countries had not fought so. Only the women of Carriol. She cast about for some question she might use to find her way here and realized how little she had prepared herself. So engrossed with getting into Time, she had given little thought to coping once there, or to an explanation for stepping out of nowhere. What plausible excuse did she have for traveling in these mountains when she did not know the customs, or where she was? Eresu knew, she was glad it was night. In the daytime she would have had some hard explaining to do, had he seen her appear suddenly from thin air.

"Not much of a talker, are you lady? Hungry? The haunch should be ready soon." The little man had a lopsided grin, and as he moved to turn the meat again, she could see he was lopsided in the way he walked, with a deep limp. He fussed about the meat, then at last settled down against a boulder. "Sit yourself down, lady. There's a log there. I am called Gravan."

She sheathed her sword and sat down astraddle the log so she could look away from the campfire, behind her. She did not give her name. That smudge of dark against the stars was tall mountains. Surely she was in the Ring of Fire.

Or on the edge of it. "The deer meat smells good," she said quietly. "The deer are plentiful?"

He gave her a puzzled look. "Scarce as teeth in a frog. Came on this one crippled." He paused, rummaged in his pack for a wineskin, took a swig and passed it across to her. "Things in those mountains that kill deer, lady. Wolves. Fire ogres. Chancy traveling for a lady," he said without malice. "Chancy—if you be traveling alone . . ."

She took a sip and handed the skin back. "I travel alone, herder." Her heart had leaped at the mention of wolves. Could there be great wolves here? Or did he mean only the common wolves? She tried to hide her eagerness. "The wolves are killers," she said casually. "Killers . . ."

He nodded, grunting, took another sip.

"Are they very bold? Do they raid your herds?"

"Sometimes, lady. We kill some, and they do not return for a while."

She let out her breath, disappointed. Common wolves, then. Only common wolves raided the herds of men. The great wolves did not.

"How do you come here, lady, traveling alone?"

"It—was silent and peaceful in the deep mountains. I—I have a sorrow, I wanted to travel in solitude." She gave him a long, deep look, eyes soulful. Her brother Jerthon would have said it made her look as if she would cry any minute. The little man nodded with quick embarrassment, obviously hoping she wouldn't burst into tears. She studied him beneath lowered lashes, trying to remember where men had ever herded goats on the mountains. The Cherban had grazed their goats on the hills of Urobb farther south, and down in the rich marsh pastures of Sangur, where few men dwelled, but not here, not on the mountains of fire. When had they come here? Surely she was in a future time—or else in a time so ancient it had been all but forgotten when she was growing up. She stared past him trying to make out more of his herd, trying to see if there were other herders.

"The village is down along that lower ridge," Gravan

offered, pointing. The moons had begun to lift in the east, fingering their gentle light across low hills. Could those be the hills of Carriol? Her pulse quickened. Or the hills along the Urobb? Running as they did, away from the mountains, they had to be one or the other. She gazed off toward the east where Carriol must lie, with a painful sweep of homesickness, thought of the twin moons rising over Carriol.

"Do you come to Dunoon with a purpose, lady?"

Dunoon? There had been no place called Dunoon in her time. And that faint rushing noise must surely be a river. A mountain river could be any one of four, but in this location, with such rounded, low hills on its east, it was either the Owdneet or the Urobb. She watched Gravan in silence. If she could know what river, she would know *where* she was, even if she did not know *when*. "I—I must confess I was lost. I saw your fire—I guess I wanted company." She unslung her waterskin and tipped it up to drink, then shook it, frowning. "Stale. Tastes of rock."

"Fill it in the river, lady. You don't seem to mind a little walk in the darkness. There," he said, pointing. "Just where that darkest ridge rises, the Owdneet flows deep and white. Sweet, good water, lady."

The Owdneet. She felt a thrill of excitement. To hear its name engulfed her at once in the fabric of her childhood, made her long for something she could not put to words. She rose slowly, casually, trying to hide her eagerness, slipped her waterskin over her shoulder and walked away toward the sound of the river; wanting to run, wanting to shout some crazy, wild welcome to the churning, ranting Owdneet.

As she drew close to the river, its roar nearly deafened her. Excited her. Her memory of the Owdneet was a memory of smells: wild tammi and sweetburrow and the smell of coolness on hot summer days. Now, though she had not yet reached the river, the smell of tammi came to her so strong it might have been crushed under her own feet passing along the bank of the river. To her left and below her, she could see the faint lights of Dunoon. It was only a tiny village, a few thatched roofs catching the moonlight. And steep down the mountain, a faint smear of light that must mark the city of Burgdeeth. This place called Dunoon lay just above Burgdeeth, then. Burgdeeth, where she had grown up. Where first she had met Ram, where they had been children together. There had been no village here on the mountain then, only the wild stag and hare, and the great wolves roaming silently. How many times had she and Ram slipped up across these meadows in secrecy to the caves of Owdneet, where the great wolves denned.

Were tyrants still in control of Burgdeeth? Was Venniver still Landmaster? Or was he long dead and turned to dust, and another Landmaster risen to rule? And what relationship was there between this herding village and Burgdeeth? She stood staring down the mountain at Burgdeeth, caught in emotions she thought had died long ago. And was there a reason why she had been drawn to this place where she and Ram had been children? Some meaningful linking to Ram here? She could see white water now, catching the moonlight, soon stood beside the river watching it plunge down the mountain. Twelve years since she had stood here. How many years, in Time, was it? How many generations?

She emptied her waterskin on the ground, then knelt and let it fill with the Owdneet's foaming brew. She drank long from her cupped hands, then rose and stood lost in the roar and beauty of the river, moonlight like white fire over its rapids. Only slowly did she become aware of another's presence, of the feeling that she was watched.

Had old Gravan followed her?

No, this was not Gravan, this presence was powerful and disturbing. She turned, drawing her sword without sound, looked back into the darkness. But something made her swing around again to stare toward the river.

She could make out nothing on the far shore but a wood, was confused, felt the presence behind her cold and waiting. She turned to face it again and sudden visions overwhelmed

26

her, a dizzying confusion of visions plunging and assailing her sense so she could not be sure what moved before her and what moved in the places of her mind. Surely what watched her was giving her the visions, for she could feel the strong sense of another being as a part of them. And then one vision came more sharply and she saw the village of Dunoon at dawn, the straw-roofed huts catching early light, herds of goats between the houses, children playing. She saw a tall, white-haired man come from one of the huts and recognized him. Anchorstar. Anchorstar, traveler in Time. Anchorstar, the last man in her time to have seen Ram. He stood beside a brightly painted wagon with two fine horses in the shafts. Then he vanished; it was night and the village was on fire, the roofs ablaze, and dark Herebian horsemen circling the burning huts, laughing.

The vision went. The night lay clear and empty, except for the presence that surely had drawn closer. The sense of something behind her across the river was gone now; only this strong, powerful being that had given her visions remained, and that being stood solidly between her and Gravan's fire.

Whatever it was, she could only face it, for if she circled, it would follow her, and if she ran it would be on her. She felt clearly it was agile and swift. The glow of Gravan's fire seemed very far away. Anyhow, what could old Gravan do to protect her that she could not do herself? She began to move away from the river, seeking in the dark, searching out for something she could attack before it attacked her.

She felt the silent laughter then, stood staring around her, frowning. Then she started toward that presence with sharp, unspoken challenge.

It laughed silently at her wariness, its voice exploding in her mind. *You need not be wary of me, sister.* A pale, huge wolf showed itself suddenly against dark boulders. But it moved into darkness again without seeming to move, was cloaked in shadows. *Was* it a wolf? Certainly no common wolf. Her pulse pounded. No common wolf could speak to her in silence. Were the great wolves here? Faw-dref's band? Was Ram here, traveling with the wolves who were his brothers? Tense with excitement, she reached out in silent speech, hoping, praying, this wolf band had to do with Ram. *Do you come from Ramad?*

*I come alone, without Ram's bidding, sister. Though he would have me here if he knew. We are far from Ramad. Far in years, sister. Far in generations. I followed you in the caves, you sensed me there. Then I followed you in Time. I was alone in the caves when I knew you wandered there. I was alone there with a sadness.* The wolf closed her mind without revealing more and slipped once more into the moonlight where Skeelie could see her deep golden coat, her wise, ageless face, the broad forehead of the great wolves, the darker stripe running from forehead to nose between wide-set golden eyes, the great breadth of shoulder. A huge wolf, carrying herself with pride and wisdom. She lifted her head to stare across at the campfire, then pulled back into shadow with, it seemed to Skeelie, more of humor than of fear as Gravan rose to stand silhouetted against the fire, his bow drawn. *Your friend has seen me, sister. He would protect his herd.* Her laughter was silent and gentle. Skeelie stepped toward Gravan, past where the wolf stood hidden.

"Slack your bow, Gravan."

But the man stood frozen, staring at the boulders waiting for the wolf to attack. The sense of him was not of fear, but only of protectiveness for his herd. Could this man, raised all his life in the protecting of the herds, stay his hand against one he thought a predator?

"This wolf will not harm your goats, Gravan."

Did Gravan know what the great wolves were? Had he ever heard of them?

The goats themselves, those battle-wise, wary bucks, had made no move of alarm. Skeelie could see three bucks standing calmly, gazing unafraid toward where the wolf stood hiding in shadow. Gravan stepped forward meaning to seek the wolf out. Skeelie raised her bow. "Lay it down, Gravan! Lay down your bow!"

Slowly he lowered his bow, watching her. When he had laid his bow aside, the wolf came out and stood crowding close to Skeelie, the great broad head pushing against Skeelie's waist. Skeelie spoke to her in silence. *How are you called? Where have you come from? Was it—was it you who opened the warp of Time for me?* Both Skeelie and the wolf watched the herder, who stood unmoving, utterly engrossed with the sight of the huge wolf that seemed as tame as a pup. Then the wolf looked up at Skeelie, her eyes appraising.

*You are very full of questions, sister. I am Torc. I moved through Time when you did, but for my own reasons. I can control Time no more than you can. In that cave were talismans, things of power that helped us. The rune. The limited powers of Cadach. Things of which you did not know. You did not know that by your very presence, by your terrible wanting and searching, you made those talismans more powerful. You did not understand Cadach's words, about the accident of your birth.*

*And you? Did you understand them?*

*I am not sure, sister. I will think on it awhile.*

Skeelie knelt, lay her head against Torc's warm shoulder, nearly weeping with the pleasure of the wolf's closeness. She felt like a child again, hugging another bitch wolf, pressing her face into the bitch's thick coat, feeling her love and power. Torc licked her arm, then raised her head. Skeelie could feel her sudden wariness, and she grew quiet too. *What is it, Torc? What do you sense? Not the herder. He is harmless.*

*There was another presence, sister, when you first went to the river. Did you not sense it when you stood beside the river? An evil presence—but perhaps it now is gone.*

Skeelie felt every sense grow taut with questioning, but could feel nothing. *There was something, Torc. I cannot sense it now. What was it?*

*I do not know how to call it. A dark shadow. It is the shadow I have followed, it is what brought me here. I must study it, sister, before I can know what it is. I do not like studying it. It sickens me.*

Skeelie stood up, glanced at Gravan who still stood frozen, staring at Torc. The moons, risen higher, cast their light across his lined face. He began to limp toward them. Skeelie tensed, for though he had laid aside his bow, surely he had a knife. She felt Torc's amusement. *I could kill him with one quick slash, sister. But he means no harm.* Skeelie saw that Gravan's face was filled with wonder now. She reached to touch his thoughts, felt his awe; his voice was filled with awe. "She is no common wolf, lady."

She hardly paused, but lied smoothly. "No, Gravan, she is not. She is quite unlike her wild brothers. I found her on the mountain and raised her from a cub." Why did she feel it necessary to be so secretive about Torc's true nature? Yet the fewer who knew what Torc was, and so what she herself must be, the safer they would remain. Only a Seer could speak with the great wolves.

"*You* trained her? A wolf from the mountains? But she is so big. She is not . . ."

"I found her orphaned. I fed her as the herb woman bid me, to make her grow large. I trained her just as I have trained horses. Folk tell me I have a gift for such, for training the dumb brutes."

She felt Torc's silent laughter.

Gravan stared at her only half-believing, then settled once more by the fire, content, it seemed, to let her words lie. He said nothing more for a long time, then at last he drew his knife and began to slice meat from the roasting haunch and lay it on thick pieces of bread. She was ravenous, found the meat tender and juicy, and did not talk for some time—though she spoke in silence to Torc. *Where are we Torc? Into what time have we come?*

*I do not know, sister. Nor do I care. I only follow the shadow.*

*But you gave me visions, back there by the river. As if you—*

*Visions that came to me, sister. I cannot say why. Some linking, something here that has to do with the powers you and Ramad have touched. Visions that came because of that power. But nebulous, sister,* she said, feeling Skeelie's rising excitement. *Ramad is not here, nor does he come here, that I can surely sense. I do not know in what time we are. You must learn that from the herder.*

Skeelie accepted another slice of bread heaped with deer meat, then began to reach into Gravan's mind. She did not receive at once any sense of time, for his thoughts were filled with the knowledge of goats, more knowledge than she wanted. Finally she began to touch on Gravan's childhood. He had come to these mountains when he was very young, she could see the child's vision of his family and the Cherban tribe making their first rude camp. Yet something more interesting lay at the edges of his mind, something shadowed, half-forgotten. Something she could not sort out unless he were to bring it directly to his own attention. Something to do with darkness, with Seers. Some old bitterness, a tribal bitterness that lay half-buried.

"Your people settled Dunoon, Gravan?"

"Yes, lady."

"And where did they come from? Why did they come to this spot?"

"Oh, from the Bay of Pelli, lady. From the marsh country."

"But why? That is fine pasture, Gravan."

"Surely you know that Pelli was all but laid waste when the Hape ruled there, lady." She stared at his mention of the Hape. "My grandparents left Pelli at that time, a young couple with small children, herding their goats, their livelihood, up into the hills of the Urobb."

Gravan's grandparents had been young, then, in the time of the Hape. In the time that she had left less than an hour ago. And his sense of darkness came from that time, from

31

tales told and retold. Fear of the Hape and of the dark Seers lay like an ancient shadow on his mind.

"After the Hape was slaughtered by the Seers of Carriol, lady, there were no more dark Seers save the one who escaped that battle. My family could have returned to Pelli, but they had not the heart. They worked their way northward up into these pastures. They were raided many times by the Herebians while they lived along the Urobb. This land, these high pastures, seemed to hold some terror for the raiding Herebian tribes. They would not come here."

So a dark Seer had escaped from the battle of the Castle of Hape. She had not known that, nor had Ram. None of them had known. He must have spun a strong mind-shielding indeed, to hide his escape as well. How had he managed it? And where had he gone? Which Seer had it been, among those dark, evil ones? "Tell me of that dark Seer, Gravin. There must be many tales of him."

Gravan produced the wineskin and passed it to her. "Surely you know, lady, how NilokEm fogged the minds of the Carriolinian warriors so they did not know he escaped, how he and his kin after him rose to power." He watched her drink, accepted the wineskin. "But of course there are no dark Seers of power any more. A handful of alley-bred street rabble, some with Seer's blood among them, that is all. There has been no power since the twin grandsons of NilokEm were defeated by Macmen, and by a mysterious warrior. It is said their grandmother was a spell-cast woman come out of some enchantment, bred by NilokEm like a ewe on the hill, then never seen more. NilokEm died some years after his son's birth, with a knife through his heart. Some say that he died by the hand of Ramad of the wolves." Gravan stopped speaking abruptly and stared at her. "What is it, lady? What did I say to startle you so?"

"Nothing, Gravan. Nothing."

"Folk tell that Ramad returned nine years after the battle of Hape, to kill NilokEm. Surely you have heard of the battle of the Castle of Hape. That is an old, old tale."

The excitement made her stomach churn. "I—have heard it. Tell me what happened after Ram—Ramad killed NilokEm. You speak every well of these things."

Gravan sipped reflectively. "The land was peaceful until the dark twins rose." He settled back against the boulder. "The twins' younger brother, Macmen, was a Seer of light, raised apart from them. It is told there was a streak of goodness come down from the grandmother. When Macmen came to power in Zandour, the dark twins were enraged by his gentle leadership and brought Pellian armies to attack Zandour. Then there came a young man, out of some spell-cast place, to fight by Macmen's side." Gravan looked across at her, caught by the wonder of the tale. "A young man with a great band of wolves by his side, lady. And the winged horses of Eresu come down out of the sky like a tide to help him. Just so did Ramad of the wolves, before him, fight at the castle of Hape, mounted on a winged horse, and with the magical wolves slaughtering the dark Seers. Wolves some say are only myth." Gravan stared at Torc, his eyes kindling with the knowledge of what Torc must surely be. Torc looked back at him blankly, then rolled over on her back with utter lack of dignity, as if she had no idea what human speech was about. Skeelie reached idly to rough her fur, hiding her apprehension at Gravan's interest. But Gravan was not put off. "*She* is one of them, lady. You— you fondle a great wolf as if she were a kitten. Only a Seer can command the great wolves, lady. You—you are of Seer's blood."

Skeelie looked back at him uneasily. But his look was only eager, filled with wonderful curiosity. What difference would it make for this little man to know the truth about her? He stared so openly, so eagerly awaiting her answer.

*Be careful, sister. Take care.*

*But he knows. It's no good lying now.*

*Then say nothing. Divert him!* Torc thought sharply.

"Surely there are Seers among your tribe, Gravan. You are of Cherban blood, the very blood of Seers."

Gravan seemed utterly in awe of her now. "Not so many Seers, lady. Not like the old times. The Seeing is not as strong as the old tales tell it once was." He could not disguise his fascination with both Skeelie and Torc. He stared at Torc until the pale wolf thought cryptically, *Oh well, the little man is harmless. He thinks I am beautiful, sister.*

Skeelie scowled at Torc, laid a hand on the wolf's broad head, gave Torc a push. *You are insufferably vain.* Then, "Who was that Seer, Gravan? The Seer who appeared so suddenly to fight by Macmen's side?"

"What folk tell is impossible, lady. Folk believe that Seer was Ramad of the wolves, returned upon Ere sixty-six years after he defeated the Hape."

Skeelie sat frozen. Ram was alive then. He moved through Time, moved through Ere's history undaunted. Somewhere Ramad lived. Or, he had been alive at least in the time of Macmen. "How long has it been, Gravan, since the battle of Macmen?"

"Why, twenty-three years, lady. But no one—no one living in Ere could help but know these things—to know all that I have told you. And you, a Seer—but forgive me, lady. I speak too freely, perhaps."

Why had Ram come out of Time to battle NilokEm, and then again to battle the dark twins? It was Telien who had drawn him into the swirling fulcrum of Time, Telien he sought, not battles. Had the very existence of the dark Seers turned him from his search for Telien? How could that be? How could he be turned aside from the search for his love? Or had he been pulled out of Time without volition? Had the power of the runestones moved him to other needs here, beyond his committment to Telien?

"And now," Gravan said, almost to himself, "now perhaps evil rises anew. Perhaps people were foolish to put off the street rabble of Pelli as of little consequence. There are rumors, now, that the Seers among that rabble may have more power than men thought. That they may be the sons of the dark twins, street-bred from whores. That perhaps they are not only tricksters and petty thieves, that maybe they are to be feared. That perhaps they are the cause of new disagreements and small skirmishes between the several countries. Even the poor senses of the few Seers in Dunoon stir sometimes to waves of evil, to a breath of darkness off somewhere among the coastal countries."

"But if this is so, if they should rise, won't Carriol march against them?"

"It is all Carriol's Seers can do to keep their own borders strong. They have no runestone now, lady. Have not had since the stone that Ramad brought out of Tala-charen was lost in the sea."

Nearly ninety years, she thought, since the stone was lost. Yet to her it was but a handful of days. She felt empty inside, lost and afraid. Everyone she knew was dead, was dust now. Her brother, Jerthon, Tayba, all the Carriolinian council. All those she had loved. All but Ram. She bent her head to her knees, swept with desolation, with a loneliness too vast to deal with, sat so in silence for some time.

He said gently, seeing her misery but not understanding it, "Carriol will shelter any who come to her lady—Seers in fear for their lives. But she will not march forth to right the wrongs across Ere, to depose the tyrants from Burgdeeth and other cities that enslave."

"If Burgdeeth is a place of slavery, Gravan, why have your people remained so close to it, on these pastures? Doesn't the landmaster try to rule you?"

"We trade with the landmaster, lady, but we keep an upper hand in that matter. And only here will the Herebian raiders not come, for fear of the old city of the gods." Gravan leaned back and grinned, showing a missing tooth. "If the landmaster becomes difficult, we disappear among the mountains for a time, and Burgdeeth is without goat meat and hides." Skeelie caught from his mind a clear picture of a hidden valley rich with grass, and at its center a lake of molten fire. A hidden place; but a place of meaning beyond anything Gravan imagined it to have. A place that she knew, instantly, she must touch. That lake—liquid fire, red as blood, reflecting a sullen sky. Reflecting more. Hinting of images she knew she must hold in her mind and examine. Gravan prattled on comfortably, but she hardly heard him. There was a message there, in that place. Perhaps a way to Ram there.

Torc raised her head to look at Gravan. The wolf held in her mind sharply the image both she and Skeelie had taken from his thoughts, the lake of flame hidden among rising hills in a valley flanked round by sharp black peaks. Yes, there was something in that place, something they must seek, something that held as vital a meaning for Torc as it held for Skeelie.

*We will go there, sister.*

*Yes, Torc, we'll go there.* But she was afraid, though she was eager to see what that place held. Would it tell her news of Ram that she could not bear to hear? She studied Gravan, hardly able to form the question she must ask, yet knowing she could not rest until she had. She watched the shadows around the fire, watched the dark red embers of painon wood pulsing with their heat, then looked back at the old man. "When—when the battle of Macmen was ended, Gravan, what do the tales tell happened to Ramad? Do they—do they tell that Ramad died there battling by Macmen's side?"

"Oh no, lady, they do not tell that." Gravan peered at her, puzzling at her interest. Why couldn't she learn to hide her feelings more carefully? "The tales tell, lady, that after the battle, Ramad stood by the side of Macmen with the great wolves around them and that—that the next minute Macmen stood alone on the silent battlefield, Ramad and the wolves gone as if the wind itself had swallowed them."

Skeelie slept that night beside Gravan's fire with her hand couched on Torc's flank, replete with roast deer meat and Gravan's mawzee bread, and perhaps more wine than was necessary. In the early dawn, while the old herder rounded up his bucks and their does to go down into the village, she made a quiet departure, wishing him well, and headed up between black peaks in the direction his thoughts had shown her, toward the lake of fire. Torc shadowed her unseen, hunting, returning now and again or speaking to her from a distance. A silent journey back into the wild mountains.

When Torc returned from her hunt at midmorning, she lay waiting for Skeelie stretched out in a patch of sunlight between black, angled boulders, licking blood from her muzzle. Two fat rock hares lay by her side. *For your noon meal, sister.* In the sharp daylight, Skeelie could see plainly that Torc had recently nursed cubs. Torc raised her head. *My cubs are dead. They were small and helpless. I had gone to hunt.*

Skeelie looked back at her, could only offer the silent sympathy that welled in her at the bitch wolf's pain.

*I will follow the creature that killed them until I destroy it.*

"What is it, that creature?"

*It is a dark, unnatural shadow dwelling within the body of a dead man. Or, a man made mindless, as good as dead. When I returned from hunting and found my cubs, found the creature crouching over them, it vanished. Disappeared, sister. I could feel it later somewhere in the caves.*

*Then, I could feel it following you. And so I followed it. I could feel it, sister, stepping into the whirling of Time as you stepped. It follows you, but I do not know why. And I will follow it, and kill it.*

A litany of hatred and suffering. Of promise by a great wolf that both frightened and heartened Skeelie. She felt the sense of the formless dark thing. It was this she had sensed in the caves and across the river. "I cannot sense it now, Torc. Not near to us."

*No, sister. But it will return. I think it follows you as mindlessly as a skabeetle seeking prey.*

"But why?"

*I do not know. It came into those deep caves blindly, seeking something there, sensing something it seemed to need. I do not know what. It was confused and weak and*

*fit only for killing cubs. But there are powers hidden within
that creature, sister. Powers that can grow. After it disappeared from my den, I felt you come. I felt it begin to
follow you. As if you, sister, held about you that which it
sought. It came here seeking you, but now it is gone again.
What do you bear, Skeelie of Carriol, that such a dark
shadow yearns after? What weapon, what magic or what
skill? Or, perhaps, what knowledge?*

Skeelie gazed into the wolf's golden eyes and did not
know how to answer. Had that creature followed her because
of Ram, thinking she would lead it to Ram? But why? Yet
well she knew that evil was attracted to Ram because of the
power of the runestones, that evil coveted those stones perhaps beyond all else. Torc's thoughts had plunged into an
abyss half of wild emotion and half of conscious thought;
and Skeelie plunged down with them through blackness to
where the sense of the shadowy creature, and of its dark,
latent powers, came cold around her.

She shook herself free of the vision at last, stared at Torc,
touched the wolf's shaggy face with need and tenderness.
And suddenly the thought of the tree man came into her mind,
his words echoing. . . . *born outside the progression of
souls—Those so born can deal with Time sufficiently.*

"What did Cadach mean, Torc? What do those words
mean? Why do I think of them now?" She knelt and laid
her head against Torc's shoulder, drew strength from Torc.
She began to feel, with Torc, the incomprehensible web of
patterns that formed life as together they reached to touch
that web, needing to trace some new strand of meaning into
their own fragile lives.

At last Skeelie rose, took up the rock hares and cleaned
them, and tied them to her belt. They started on up between
black cliffs, pushing deep into the mountains as the afternoon sunlight thinned behind them, sending long shadows
up the lifting peaks of the Ring of Fire.

# Chapter Three

JAGGED PEAKS surrounded them. The afternoon sky grew gray and chill. The way was narrow between black cliffs, then sometimes only a ledge above a sheer drop, so Skeelie's fear of height held her tense, and she must force herself on with stubborn will. Once as they rounded a narrow bend, Torc's interest quickened, but was masked at once, leaving Skeelie uneasy. Torc stopped and turned to look at her. *I do not hide anything, sister. I try only to calm my hatred. The shadow is there in that place, come there before us. I will kill it there.* She let Skeelie feel the wild fury that drove her. Skeelie drew back, chastened, and followed Torc in silence.

They came on the valley without warning. One minute they were squeezing between black rock walls, and the next they stood staring down past their feet to a valley cupped out of the cliffs, far below. Its edge was brilliant green where grass pushed against the cliffs, but it was bare and rocky at the center, and there lay the lake of fire, a pool red as blood seeping up out of the rock, like a wound upon the land. Skeelie remembered too vividly the burning lava river inside Tala-charen, where a wolf had nearly died, remembered lava belching from mountains down over the fields to burn beasts and men alike. What kept this lava from rising continuously out of the earth to spill over its banks? The flow seemed to her to have halted only temporarily, as if it must soon rise strongly again and drown the valley.

As they made their way down the steep cliff, the wolf's silence seemed a barrier between them; then Torc turned quite suddenly, went leaping up a cliff on the left and soon was out of sight. There was no contact between them, but Skeelie knew she was not meant to follow. Was Torc leaving her? Going on her own way alone, too intense with the need to kill to follow the slow descent that Skeelie must take? Skeelie could not tell what she, herself, sensed in this wild place. As she descended the steep cliff, she began to feel the lake's hot breath, heavy and oppressive. When she stood at last close above the wide belt of grass that brushed against the rocky cliffs, she could see the dark mouths of half a dozen caves, below and to her left. She started along toward them, drawn, curious. Then suddenly Torc was before her, ears flattened and eyes flaming, baring her teeth. Skeelie backed away from her until she struck the cliff behind. *Stay hidden, sister, there are men!*

*Where, Torc? How many?* She strained to hear voices, but could make out nothing, see no movement against the back cliffs. Had sensed nothing.

*Beyond that outcropping, at the end of the valley. Five men. Come, I will show you.* Torc led her through a narrow cleft between jagged rock, toward the head of the valley. They stood at last, hidden and silent, watching five riders below them. Now she sensed them, evil and primitive, steeped in some lusting need she could not make out. Four were broad, heavy men, dark and bearded, dressed in fighting leathers. Herebian warriors. The fifth was a thin, pale creature, mounted, but with his hands bound behind him and his horse on a lead. Skeelie felt the cruelty of all five; felt the primitive strength of the warriors, and the weak, groveling avarice of the thin creature. Torc's head was lowered as for attack, her ears flat, her expression predatory and cold, her mind seeking out to read the shadowy creature, to understand its nature. *That is the one I follow, sister, that cold shadow of a man mindless and unliving. He is death, inhabiting the body of a man. I do not understand how. The ancient Seers would have called such a wraith, sister. One of living death. He seeks something here. Seeks something even as I seek him. He has abandoned following you, sister, for something he seeks more. And the greedy Herebians have seen his need and made him captive through his own lusting weakness. They seek what he seeks, they seek a treasure here.*

Skeelie could feel it now, the sense of the riders having been drawn to this place. What power had this valley to draw them? What did they seek? And what did she herself seek? She watched them dismount, felt the captive begin to quest out, intent, searching out blindly, then sniffing, turning its face from side to side.

Torc's eyes glinted, her lips pulled back in the silent snarl of a killer. Skeelie laid her hand on Torc's rough shoulder and opened her mind wider to the great wolf, nearly reeled with Torc's hatred and with the force of evil that Torc's senses touched from the wraith. They stood pressed together, girl and wolf, strung tight; then Torc left her, began to creep forward between the stone cliffs.

*Don't Torc! Four armed warriors. . . .* But Torc did not pause, and Skeelie followed her, sword drawn. They descended in silence, stood at last just above the men, so close that Torc could have leaped down onto any one of the horses and killed it. Skeelie felt the mind-shield that Torc placed against the beasts, so they did not sense her. The warriors had begun to prod the wraith impatiently; then they made it kneel. It began to crawl, snuffling at the ground like a hunting weasel, inching along smelling the dirt, changing direction again and again in search of some illusive scent, its thin body making jerky movements, its resemblance to a man all but gone. Was it something other than human, in human shell? It doubled back, then thrust forward with an oily, reptilian motion, as if it had found a scent at last; groveled against its tether toward the caves.

*What does it search for, Torc?*

But Torc stood tense, her thought only a thin breath of meaning. *Do not speak, sister. Not even in silence. That one has Seer's blood.* Skeelie felt Torc's shielding of thought and tried to push out with a shield of her own, but felt clumsy and uncertain, as if the very unhealthiness of the creatures had laid a fog upon her mind. She watched

Torc creep forward, felt the wolf's cold readiness to attack. She followed, knowing this was madness; began to sense shadows from the creature's mind, to feel the vague shape of that for which it searched: something small and heavy, something buried deep. She could feel the creature's lust for that treasure.

She had a vision then of the wraithlike creature as it had stood beside the river Owdneet in darkness, watching her drink. Yes, it had sensed an aura about her, something it wanted, but she could not make out what. But then suddenly it had turned away, drawn to another trail, had followed the four Herebians who moved silently up the mountains searching—searching for what? The vision went dull and faded, left her with only the sense of the wraith sniffing and whispering around the Herebians, caught in its own mysterious greed. Skeelie could see clearly how the Herebians had stripped their pack animal, distributed the packs among the five horses and forced the wraith to mount; and the wraith, eager to search, had not resisted very strongly. She watched it now, knew that it sensed some power buried within this mountain, for it was pulling ahead eagerly toward the largest of the caves.

What did it search for? What lay there among the caves, whispering out such an essence of power that the creature seemed unable to resist?

And then she knew what it searched for, with a sudden sense that shocked her. Something small and heavy, something buried deep. She sensed the creature's lust for that treasure: a jagged, heavy treasure, shining green, roughly broken, carved with the fragments of an ancient rune.

Treasure of all treasures. That loathsome creature searched for, snuffled after, a shard of the runestone of Eresu.

Three Herebians followed it. They had lit a lamp, held it high. Skeelie could feel their greed; and feel something more from them. *Why are they afraid, Torc? They burn the lamp so brightly. Can't you feel their fear?*

*It has to do with the gods, sister. A fear bred of Herebian memory of the ancient caves of the gods. They fear the caves, fear the very mountains of the Ring of Fire. And sister, fear, in those selfish minds, makes them even the more cruel and bloodthirsty.*

*I can never understand their evil, Torc, or why I feel they are different from other men of Ere—different somehow in the very facts of their birth, their beginnings.*

*All souls born upon Ere are not of an age, sister. Some have lived many times on other planes. Some are new and untried. Some, perhaps, come upon Ere with a wash of evil already sucked into their natures, from willfully embracing past evils.*

The men pushed fearfully into the cave, the lamp burning brightly. The fourth Herebian remained behind, holding the five horses. Torc moved without sound; Skeelie crept close behind her, knowing that they could die here, that she could die fighting these men and never find Ram. But she would not abandon Torc. Torc's hatred, her lust to kill the wraith, was overpowering. When the bitch stopped suddenly and drew back with one motion to lie flat beside Skeelie, Skeelie dropped down, too. Their faces were so close she could feel Torc's warm breath, smell her musty smell. *What do you sense? Why—you're afraid, Torc!* For suddenly Torc's whole, intense being was caught in some horror that Skeelie could not fathom. She touched the wolf's shoulder. *What is it, Torc? What can make you afraid?*

*I cannot kill him, sister. I dare not. Feel out, feel out and sense what I sense, and tell me I am wrong.*

Skeelie lay still, sensing the snuffling creature, trying to become one with it against all her instincts; though she shielded herself from it. She began to feel its physical weakness, the exhausted limits of its weak body. She felt the rough, rocky earth over which it crawled, smelled earth and the dampness of the cave. Then quite suddenly and with cold terror, she knew the nature of the creature in sharp

43

detail. Sharp as pain came the knowledge, the reality of what it was.

She understood that Torc *must* not kill it.

For this creature could not die. Only its body would die. The evil within would, at the body's death, be set free to take the body of another.

*The body of a Seer, sister.*

There were no Seers there among the Herebian warriors.

*You are the only Seer, Skeelie of Carriol. If I kill that creature, its dark, fetid soul will enter into your body. And you cannot prevent it.*

*I would fight it, Torc! I—*

*You cannot fight this. I think it is too steeped in evil. It is a dead soul that can never die again. I think it would possess you. It . . . without a body to possess, it would slowly fade into nothing. In that sense, I suppose it would die. But you cannot kill it. If a human tries, it will possess him. You must go away from here, sister. If* they *kill it, after it finds the runestone, it will come to possess you.*

*I will not go away. It searches for a shard of the rune-stone. If it should find such, I must somehow take that shard. For Ram—for all of Ere. I could not leave a shard of the runestone.*

The Herebian beside the cave's entrance tipped up a wineskin to drink. He held the five horses carelessly, their reins tangled in one hand. Torc watched him with cold appraisal. *I could kill him with no trouble, the fat Herebian. Make one less to battle later, if the shard is found.*

Skeelie tried to sense the men inside the cave, but now no sense came clear except that of the wraith. The guard drank again. Skeelie took off her pack to make movement easier, laid it beside her quiver and bow behind a boulder. Then she started forward behind Torc, her hand on her sword.

*He has heard you, sister.*

*I made no noise.*

*He heard something, he's looking up. He's coming.* Torc crouched, ready to spring.

*Don't let him see you, Torc!*

Torc glanced at her with disdain.

*If he sees you, he will know you are a great wolf, and so know me for a Seer just as Gravan did. If he finds me alone, maybe . . .*

But Torc's fury exploded, the wolf flew past her in a streak of dark violence as the warrior came up the last rise. She hit him so quickly he could not cry out, pinned him, her teeth deep in his throat as he fell, his only sound a gurgle of expended breath.

He lay still beneath Torc's weight, twisted once, then went limp. Blood gushed from his throat. The left shoulder of his tunic bloomed with spreading red stain as if a red flower opened. Torc turned to stare back at Skeelie, then spun away from the man, crouching anew, a snarl deep in her throat. Skeelie swung around, her sword challenging sword as a warrior towered over her, come silently out of the cave, perhaps at the small noise of scuffling; and he followed by another, so the two drove Skeelie back. Then one spied Torc, sheathed his sword and drew arrow. *Get away, Torc! Get away!* The wolf spun, leaped to disappear among boulders seconds before the arrow loosed. Skeelie parried one broad sword, then two, could not summon power to touch the wolf's mind, so occupied was she; felt the sting of a blade, was backed against the cliff. Saw Torc leap on one of the warriors; and she was battling only one Herebian as the other rolled against her feet locked in fierce embrace with the snarling wolf. The Herebian swung his heavy sword at her like a battering ram. His dark face filled her vision, filled her mind. Black beard, stinking leathers. She dodged, plunged her blade at the man's leather-clad belly, and felt her sword swept away, felt a dull blow along her neck, a fist across her face. She was falling, twisted with pain. Knew no more.

\* \* \*

SHE WOKE, was lying on rocky ground, her hands tied behind her, her feet tied. She ached all over, as if she had been dragged down the cliff. Her sword was gone, the silver sword Ram had forged for her. She stared at the empty sheath, then tried to roll over, pushed against stone, lifted her head to see she was lying against a boulder at the mouth of the cave. She could hear voices from the darkness, could not make out the words. When she twisted around, pain clutched at her like fire. She stared into the dark cave. Faint light moved there, and a voice rose shouting with anger, the words muffled by echoes. Another man swore—garbled, choppy sounds. Then a thin, querulous voice that must be the wraith's. "I cannot! It is not the same! Not the same!" Shaking voice, nearly weeping. "I swear it! I swear!"

"*This* is all you found! We came into the wretched cave for *this?*" A dull shattering, as if something had been thrown against the cave wall and broken. She felt dizzy, could not bring a vision or make sense of the exchange. The whining of the wraith pulled her back.

"I swear there is nothing, I swear. It is buried in a mountain, maybe not this mountain, maybe . . ."

"You'll search every mountain in the Ring. You'll find it, or die looking."

"It lies to the west, perhaps. Lies deep in a mountain, I promise . . ."

Tala-charen? Did the wraith sense a shard of the rune-stone lying buried beneath Tala-charen, as she and Ram had always thought? It cried out in pain. The Herebian shouted. "Get up or I'll kick you again!" Then, "Fetch the horses, BolLag! Why didn't Stalg tie them before he—never mind, just catch them! We're heading to the west reaches. Worse luck those two clods got themselves killed. If you see that wolf again, slaughter it."

Feet went by her. Large and heavily booted. She kept her eyes closed, did not move. "What about the wench?" the man called back.

"Throw her over StaIg's saddle. He won't be riding again."

"She's no good to us. What do we need her for?"

"Stupid dolt. She's female, ain't she!"

The feet went on. She could hear sounds as if he were gathering up the horses. The other warrior came out, leading the wraith. It paused to look into her face. She kept her eyes closed, could feel its interest like a lance. When it continued to stare, she could not help but open her eyes. Its face was loose over the bones. Its pale, dead eyes were sunken deep, the whites gone yellow. Eyes dark-ringed, expressionless, looking deep inside her, seeing things she did not want it to see. The cold sense of the creature gripped her. She stifled the need to cry out, turned her face away from it with horror. What was this thing, dwelling in a man's body?

The thing crawled on at last, but pulled constantly against its lead back toward the darkness. The Herebian kicked it to move it along, then bound it to a boulder and left it; then he returned to stand over Skeelie.

"Get up!"

She lay as if unconscious.

The man grabbed her by the shoulder and flung her up like a bag of meal, scraping her bound hands beneath her across the rocky wall. He pushed her against the wall, and when she struggled, he hit her hard. She lunged at him, bit his hand, then crouched, doubled with pain when he struck her in the stomach.

"Not the sort of female *I* relish," the one called BolLag said.

"Female's female, What's the difference. Throw her over the saddle and tie her down good. I'll take the fight out of her tonight."

"But she'll only slow us HaGlard. What—"

"Hoist 'er!"

Skeelie was thrown across a saddle face down, her head hanging. The horse shied and snorted, then went still and trembling, as if it would bolt any minute. The breath was knocked out of her. The saddle pressed deep into her ribs, smelled of rancid oil. She could feel Torc somewhere close by, gauging her position, gauging her best angle of attack. *Don't Torc! Wait until they separate. Follow us, Torc, and wait!* The man called HaGlard had said westward. Would they carry her in the direction of Tala-charen? But maybe she needn't wait, for they had not tied her to the saddle yet, though her hands and feet were tied and she felt nearly helpless, belly down across the horse. Still, the Herebian who held the reins had turned away to tend another mount. Her horse was nervous, trembling at its strange burden: it would take little to make it leap away. To make it run. She could sense Torc slipping closer, then could feel the wolf's tenseness as she crouched.

*Now, sister! Gig it! Gig it!*

She kicked the animal's shoulder, its belly. It screamed and leaped away, nearly dumping her. BolLag cried out, swearing, as the reins were jerked from his hand. Skeelie clung to the saddle, her ribs bruised, as the terrified horse crashed through tall grass along the cliff. She could feel turmoil behind her, knew that Torc had leaped for a horse's throat. It was all she could do to cling, to balance on the plunging horse. She could hear another horse running.

She felt Torc behind her at last. Felt Torc swerve, sensed an arrow released. She heard a horse scream, twisted around in the saddle enough to glimpse a riderless horse careening away. Her own horse spun, nearly spilling her, and began to scramble in terror up the boulders. She was slipping, tried to sense what was happening. *Torc! Torc!* Felt Torc leap and pull at her. *Now, sister! Now!* She slid off the crazed horse nearly under its hooves, rolled free as it plunged away, and lay still among boulders, hurting all over, trying to collect her senses.

She felt Torc's warm breath on her wrist, Torc's teeth, as the bitch-wolf chewed at the rope.

Skeelie's hands were free. She bent to untie her feet, struggled with ropes, jerked them loose at last, and they leaped together up the side of the cliff and began to climb, Torc slowing, waiting for her as, behind them, a rider drew bow. They slipped behind rock. Skeelie heard the two men running over gravel. "There, HaGlard, they climb there!" She ran blindly, following Torc, trusting Torc's keener senses as the wolf swerved into a cave, ran in darkness. She was terrified of being trapped there weaponless, could hear the Herebians gaining, was panting with fear as running footsteps echoed close behind, then felt Torc swerve back to attack—but there was sudden silence behind them.

Torc had stopped, stood listening, feeling out.

Low voices slurred by echo against the cave walls into senselessness. But voices coming closer in the formless dark. *They have no light, sister. They have left the lantern or lost it. Help me—help me bring a vision upon them, for they fear the dark caves.*

Together, Torc and Skeelie brought darkness down thicker and deeper than the cave's darkness, darkness with the sense of gods in it. The Luff'Eresi towered, winged creatures half-man and half-horse, violent in their power and righteousness, brought their fury into the cave, so their hatred of the weak and twisted filled the cave with an awesome thundering power, so real and frightening that Skeelie wondered afterward if she and Torc alone had wrought such splendor and felt that they had not. Felt that what they had formed there was aided by something unknown.

They sensed the warriors' fear, felt them stumble and turn; heard them running out of the cave. Skeelie felt Torc's silent wolfish laugh. *A fine vision, sister. Fine. They search for their horses now. They will leave us, never fear. And the terror of our vision will follow them. And I—I will follow them. I must follow them.*

They stood together, just inside the dark entrance to the cave, and watched the two Herebians drive their horses to a central point against the cliffs and capture them. Watched them strip the dead horse of its gear, then force the captive wraith up onto one of the animals and tie him to the saddle.

Skeelie did not want to think of Torc leaving her, but the bitch wolf must do as she had committed herself to do.

*When it is away from you, when it can no longer enter your body, I can kill it, sister.*

"But you said, if it is freed from that body it will take another. Become more powerful. The Herebians are strong, they—"

*They must separate when they make camp, to hunt, to gather wood, to see to the horses. I will follow until I can kill them both, one at a time. Then only the wraith will be left, and when I kill it, it will wander bodiless and so grow weak. It cannot enter into me, it has not that power, sister. That shadow killed my cubs. If I do not kill it, I will cripple it so it finds the body useless, yet cannot escape it.*

The riders headed up toward the west side of the valley, hurrying their horses. Torc's very spirit seemed to follow them, heavy and predatory. *Ramad would bid me stay with you, sister, but I cannot. Ramad is not here to bid.* The bitch wolf's eyes never left the receding figures as they urged their horses up between the rocky cliffs. *I must trail that darkness, sister, and destroy it.*

Skeelie knelt, put her arms around Torc's shaggy neck, pressed her face into the bitch-wolf's golden coat. The great wolves had comforted her and Ram in their childhood, were her security in a deep, indestructible way. She felt tears come, hugged Torc hard. The wolf's warmth and strength flowed through her; the bitch-wolf licked her neck, took her arm between killer's teeth, gently, in a timeless salute.

Then Torc was gone down across the valley past the molten lake, leaping through the grass on the far side of the valley, then up the cliffs until she was lost from view. Gone in one instant. Gone.

Skeelie turned away at last, annoyed at herself for feeling such loss. Torc did what she had to do.

Skeelie made her way along the rim of the valley to where the two Herebians lay dead, retrieved her pack and bow, her arrows, searched for her sword, knowing well she would not find it, and cursed the Herebians sharply. It was lucky she had hidden her pack and bow. She searched the dead warriors for sword or knife, but their friends had stripped them of everything useful. At last she entered the cave where the wraith had crawled and snuffled and began to search for what it had found there, striking her flint over and over until she had collected eight pieces of what looked like a small clay bowl. It puzzled her, for there seemed indeed to be a power about it. She climbed the cliff to some 'stunted trees, gathered pitch on a sharp rock, and stuck the pieces together: a bowl with a small, useless base. Then, with rising excitement she turned the bowl over and saw that it was not a bowl at all, but a bell. What had seemed the base was a part of the broken handle. She held the bell on her open palm, lightly, and memories flooded back to her. Ram had grown up in a house of bells, hundreds of bells collected by Gredillon, she who had raised him and taught him his Seer's skills. Had this bell something to do with Ram? Did it hold some message for her? Had it led her here? In Gredillon's house of bells, the wolf bell had stood on the mantel, presiding over Ram's birth, and with it he had learned to call down the jackals and foxes before ever he spoke to the great wolves.

The strength of this bell was what the wraith had felt and thought it the runestone, though there was little comparison. The bell had a power, but not like the runestone of Eresu.

Still, it spoke to her. She closed her eyes and let it bid her. It made no vision, but led her directly, gently, to the fiery lake with so strong a bidding that she hardly saw the rocky ground, saw little clearly until she stood on the lake's shore, staring down at the blood-red lava. The heat was intense and soon nearly unbearable, so she ripped open her collar, then at last removed her tunic.

The vision came suddenly, turning the lake black as jet, and she saw Ram reflected in a brief flash of battle, his face smeared with blood and his mouth open in a silent shout. Then the lake grew red and boiling again. As if she had dreamed and was only now awakening, something shouted silently, *Open your mind, Skeelie. Open your mind and look*. She tried to see deeper, then closed her eyes at last and let herself float on the incredible heat, letting go, felt a calm take her and opened her eyes to feel cool wind above the red lake. Then the colors of lake and mountains began to dim, to soften, and the sky to grow iridescent, the grass along the cliffs to turn silvery. And mists were blowing across the lake forming the shapes of creatures, shimmering, animals crowding all around her, mythical animals, a silver triebuck, a pale snow tiger, animals she could not afterward remember, all cream and silver and pale-hued. At first they did not move or blink. Then one shifted, its movement so slight she was not sure she had seen movement. Another turned its head deliberately to stare at her, but the motion was so smooth it might have been only shifting light. And yet it stared, its eyes like translucent moons.

And then came a great dark lumbering animal pushing between the others. It was all movement and weight, was neither bear nor bull, but so strangely made that it seemed both of these. It came shouldering up to Skeelie, smelling of musky deep places half-forgotten and carrying heat about it, a breath of musky heat. She could see the ridges and roughness of its coarse-haired hide. It knelt before her suddenly and clumsily.

She knew she was meant to mount. She watched its little dark eyes. A shudder rippled her skin. She took up her pack, her bow. The beasts stood watching, silver and tawny pale, the great dark animal like a misshapen mountain patiently awaiting her.

She mounted at last, swung up onto the beast's broad, warty back and settled herself into its heavy folds of rough skin. It wheeled with her, and the wind caught her face; she saw the other animals wheel in a blaze of silver, lifting into the wind, lifting through white space. Valley and lake vanished in a blur. Space was light, and light was Time, and nothing existed but this moment endless across wind, careening, wind tearing at her.

The animal's body was warm, but her pack and bow were like ice against her back. Her hands gripped the warty skin along its neck. They sped through space, leaped winds. Time melted into one great wind, and she rode at its center, her blood pounding in her ears. The pale beasts crowded against her legs in their headlong flight, their wind-torn breath warming her. Once the great dark beast turned its head to look back at her, and its eyes shone white and wild in that dark, ugly face.

They sped through a world of ice and crystal and pale shadows. Pastel-tinted waters slid past against pale hills. White sunsets rose before them like great diamonds, and on they sped. The animals' occasional clash of hoofbeats over rock was like the sound of jewels spilled on marble. Time was the wind rushing past them in tearing waves, showing now a bloody snatch of battle, now a peaceful village, all vanishing at once. A face, a woman crying out, a scene of death. All gone at once.

Then suddenly, with no change of motion, the beast had ceased to move. He stood still upon a ridge of craggy stone. Skeelie sat staring dumbly about her, realized they were still, realized that the wind had stopped, the flight stopped. The pale beasts stood silently around her and then began to fade. Her own steed was fading; she must slide down, must not fade with them.

She dismounted, shaky and unsteady, stood staring helplessly as the beasts became thin and transparent. They shimmered as if they were seen through water; then they were gone.

She stood alone on a mountain path in bright midmorning.

The sense of wild flight and of terrible cold, and of the beast's warmth and its musty scent, clung about her. Midmorning in what time? A path in what place?

# Chapter Four

SHE STOOD ON A NARROW, rocky trail. Far below her sprawled a city, and beyond it gleamed them pale smear of open water. The Bay of Pelli? The Bay of Sangur? Or could it be the wilder sea beyond Carriol? At the thought of Carriol her heart contracted with longing. Could that city be part of Carriol, a city grown beyond her wildest dreams? No, from the position of the sun she must be looking south toward the Bay of Pelli. And this mountain was far too close to the coast to be a part of the Ring of Fire. It could only be Scar Mountain, standing just above Zandour. Scar Mountain, where Ram had been born; and like a whisper the tree man's words touched her, stirred her, *Follow the source of Ramad's beginning. Touch the place of his childhood and his strength.*

Could this be the time of Ram's childhood? The thought excited and terrified her. Up this narrow path would she find Gredillon's house carved into the side of the mountain? Find the young Ramad there, a child, as she had first known him? Would his Seer's skills tell him that she would one day be his friend, in time still ahead of him? She started up the path with bent head, uncertain in her emotions. Was she afraid to see Ram so, small and vulnerable? She felt very tired suddenly, almost weak. She realized she was hungry and could not remember when she had last eaten. Early morning beside Gravan's campfire? No, she remembered cooking rock hares on the mountain. That seemed a lifetime ago. She turned a bend in the path, thinking of her empty stomach, and came on the stone house abruptly. Stone slabs against the mountain, heavy timber door.

It was just as Ram had shown her in their childhood visions. Inside, she would find it carved deep into the mountain, half-house, half-cave. And its walls would be all carved into shelves where stood hundreds of bells wrought of amber and clay and amethyst, of tin and of precious glass and bronze. How often, when he waked from nightmares, had Ram yearned after his home, yearned for Gredillon? Was the bell woman here, waiting for her to push open the door just as she had waited for Ram's mother before Ram was born? Was Ram here?

She remembered the clay bell in her hand then. But her fist was tight, and when she opened her palm, only clay dust lay there. Had she shattered it in the excitement of the wild ride? In her tense climb up the mountain? She could not remember. Or had it shattered itself, when its mission was done? She mourned its loss, felt a strange fear because she could not remember when she had last held it lightly, when she had clenched her fist so tight. She did not like to be unable to account for her actions. She knocked and waited, knocked again, and then with sudden impatience, almost with fear, she flung the door open and lurched inside, hastily pushing it to behind her.

The room was very dim, with only small, shuttered windows to light it, the shutters partly broken, with some of the heavy slats hanging crooked. There were plates on the table, and chairs pulled out as if a meal had just been finished. But the food was petrified into dry greenish lumps; and a layer of dust thick as gauze covered plates, table, the chairs and beds, covered shapeless litter scattered across the floor, heaps of rags or clothes, and the scattered bits of what she made out to be broken bells, as if someone had pulled them from the shelves in a rage and flung them on the stone floor. She remembered then, Ram telling of his father's fury when he came searching for Ram and could not find him; how he had torn this house apart, searching. She remembered Ram's words suddenly and sharply. Ancient scenes began to rise out of the dust, and voices to speak in the room. She was immersed suddenly and wholly in Ram's childhood, immersed in joy, in pain, in a dozen scenes, sweeping her through those painful, growing years until she was a child again herself, loving Ram with all her child's soul.

She stood, drained at last, with tears running down her cheeks. The room loomed dim and gray around her. Now that she knew this part of Ram's life, knew it too well, the pain of it would never leave her.

Near the hearth lay a small boy's tunic, its shape plain under the blanket of dirt. She knelt to pick it up, and it fell apart in her hands. When she touched the cover of one of the three cots, the thread disintegrated under her exploring fingers. She shivered, hugging herself, trying to drive out the cold. If she went down into the city of Zandour, which lay below this mountain, would she find it dead and moldering, too?

Or if Zandour were a city still alive, would she hear talk of a long-dead Ramad of the wolves?

She had a strong desire to clean this room, to sweep away the dust and collect the broken bells, make it clean and livable. Perhaps to stay here awhile. But in hopes of what? That Ram would come to her in this long-lost place? She looked at the petrified food on the table with distaste, at the dusty bed.

She knew she must sleep, she was achingly tired, but did not find the thought of sleeping in this room very pleasant, because of the decay, because of the painful scenes the room seemed still to contain. A cold draft touched her, and she tightened the latch on the door, wished for her sword. She turned back the bedcover at last, managing to make only one tear in it. The blanket beneath seemed sturdy enough, though it smelled of ancient things. Darkness drifted through her mind, as if the dust itself drugged her. She fell onto the bed and curled around, knees bent, her arm over her bow and pack.

She slept deeply. Not until hours later did the dreams begin to push around her, to touch on moments of Ram's life, to form a pattern that, afterward, she could not reconstruct, but which left her somehow strengthened. As if she had touched powers basic to Ram and touched a meaning central to all life.

She woke to a gray, dim morning, hungry because she had not eaten the night before, angry at herself for not taking better care. She sat up, fuzzy with sleep, the night dreams hardly separated from the gray shadows of the room, and began to rummage in her pack for food. A small sound stopped her. The door latch was lifting.

She snatched up her bow, pushing cobwebs from her mind, as the door pushed noiselessly in.

Dull gray light crept in through the widening crack, the same flat gray that seeped in around the broken shutters. She waited, arrow to bow, her heart pounding, sleep cast aside. What was that smell? Like something dead.

Then she saw the hand feeling in through the crack of the door. A thin, white hand. The dead smell increased, was sickening. A shadow blocked the widening crack. The door pushed in in one quick movement, and a dark figure stood looking in at her, a faceless silhouette. A figure slight as a twig.

When it turned, she could see the side of its face: pale, skull-thin. Its cape was bloodstained; blood lay smeared across its cheek, down its side and arm. It stood watching her. And she knew it had come here to die. Had followed her, meant to take her body in place of its own dying one.

Why her? Why had it sought her? Across what span of Time had it come seeking, and what had wounded it so badly? And where was Torc? What had happened to Torc, who had gone so confidently to follow and destroy the wraith? She felt a twisting fear for Torc; and a fear for herself that made her go sick with apprehension. *It is a dead soul that can never die again.* The memory of Torc's words made her shiver. *It would possess you.* She longed to kill it and knew she dare not do so.

She made her mind seek out, listening, until at last her inner Seer's sense touched the essence of the wraith. Its dark image came around her, lusting to drive out her spirit, lusting for the shell of her body, for her skills. Images of torture crowded in from its mind. Then she felt the pain of a sword across the wraith's cheek, was swung into sudden battle. A dark, familiar Herebian raider slashed at its shoulder, and she felt the wraith's pain. Then the Herebian HaGlard attacked his brother, and she did not understand what they fought for among themselves.

She saw Ram suddenly, slipping inward toward the battle unseen, and caught her breath. Ram, preparing to attack the Herebians. Her heart pounded at the sight of him. He moved stealthily, his red hair in shadow. Ram, linked with the Herebians who had captured the wraith; surely linked with the wraith itself. But why? What had happened to bring them together across Time and space?

Ram was almost on the battle but still unseen, then one of the warriors glimpsed him and turned from fighting to attack him. She watched with drawn breath, willing her power against the Herebians as both swords were raised against Ram. And she knew, suddenly and sharply, what they fought over, what Ram sought.

The Herebians had found a shard of the runestone. A shard sniffed out by the wraith from beneath the mountain Tala-charen. But she was seeing a vision past; seeing, from the wraith's mind, what had already happened to it, for the wraith itself moved in the room behind her. She jerked suddenly from the vision and spun to face it, her fury drowning fear, her fury at what it had intended for Ram.

The wraith had waited, on the edge of that battle, waited for Ram to die. Its cold desire for Ram's death sickened her. She stared at its white, bloody face and lunged suddenly, grabbed it, sickened by its stench. It spun. She kneed it in the belly, so it fell screaming, and she was on it again, hitting it across the neck so it cowered away from her in pain. She stood over it, trembling with fury. She sensed the battle, sensed Ram fighting for his life against the two Herebians while the wraith waited for him to die. She saw Ram fall, saw HaGlard draw sword over Ram, then the vision went foggy or she dizzy, she did not know which. She was so confused, was wild with anxiety for Ram. She shook the wraith, screaming. "Is he dead? Did he die there?" But the wraith only looked at her, cold and expressionless. She shook it again, hit it so hard it screamed, gurgling, fighting unconsciousness with cold hatred. Ram could not be dead, or the wraith would have taken his body. She pulled the wraith up, nauseated at its closeness, tried to see again that other time, glimpsed for an instant something lying in the dust of that time, trampled by the boots of fighting men. Something shining green. Saw a hand reach for it in shadow, then the wraith was unconscious and the vision gone.

RAM KNIFED a Herebian and spun away as the man fell. He saw the runestone gleaming in the dust at his feet for one instant, then kicked aside. He searched wildly and could not find it. As the other Herebian bore down on him, wounded and uncertain, he turned and killed the man. The wraith groveled beside the first body, then was gone. Vanished. And with it, the runestone was gone.

He stood shaken, staring at emptiness where the wraith had been, where the runestone had been. Clouds of Time swirled around him and he felt then as he had felt when he first sensed the stone here through the thoughts of the wraith. He had trailed those thoughts. But he had battled and killed the Herebians only to see the stone snatched from the dust beneath his feet. He stood staring at the two dead bodies, hardly seeing them, stricken at his stupid, senseless loss of the runestone.

And stricken at the escape of the wraith. He should have killed it. For he saw it suddenly and clearly in the vision of a dim, shuttered room rimed with dust; and he saw the figure it faced.

How had it come there to the room he knew so well? How, out of all possibilities, had Skeelie come there? Why?

*Why?* He felt her cold fury sharply as she faced the wraith; then felt her terror.

How had Skeelie crossed the barrier into Time? Why had she? Had she been flung so, against her will? Or had she, stubborn Skeelie, somehow crossed the barrier on purpose? He did not want to ask himself why.

In what time was she, then, in that moldering stone house? And why had the wraith gone to her? Ram reached out to her, but could no more guide himself to her than to Telien. The wraith had the runestone now and would surely be the more powerful because of it. What *was* that creature? Was it linked to the same evil as the dark Seers? As the Hape? Was all evil linked in some patterning of forces he could not yet comprehend? Surely that evil touched Skeelie. He forced his powers out blindly across Time to drive the wraith away from her. But he felt as clumsy and helpless as a babe.

SKEELIE STOOD staring across the littered room at the wraith as it regained consciousness, but her thoughts were all of Ram. Was Ram injured, badly hurt? She could touch no vision now from the wraith's mind. Had it taken the runestone? If it had, did that mean that Ram did indeed lie wounded?

The wraith opened its eyes, watched her coldly. She felt its longing for death, knew it wanted her to kill it. It rose slowly and, without changing its expression, began to stalk her. She backed away from it, bow drawn. It shuffled toward her. She spun, pushed the table at it, twisting, and knocked the wraith flat. It lay writhing beneath the upturned table for some moments before it rose, and again moved toward her. Its shoulder drooped now, and its wounded arm hung loose. It moved silently and steadily with hatred so strong she thought hatred alone might stifle her breath. It began to whisper hoarsely. She could not at first make out the words. Was it saying, *Our way?* Yes. "*Our* way. *Our* way," over and over. Its voice was dull and muted, insistent as a heartbeat. Perhaps its voice replaced the heartbeat, in the emptiness of that inhuman void. "*Our* way. *Our* way. *Our* way. You will come into me *our* way, as the others have come. You will be part of us. We will live in you. Healthy. Young. We will have strength in you, strength . . ." It ended hissing, pushed toward her, its bony hands reaching.

She backed away from it. Its eyes never left her, never blinked. She glanced around the room, searching for anything that might help her. How could you fight something you dared not kill? Her hands trembled. She brought all the strength of her mind to bear against it. But her Seer's power seemed not to touch it. She began to lose her nerve.

Stop it, Skeelie! Kill it if you must, then battle its dark spirit! But don't *quail* before it! You've killed Herebian soldiers. What makes you afraid now? The dark, she thought, quailing in spite of herself. The death-face, the cold evil that it stinks of. She backed away, her eyes never leaving it, her arrow taut in the bow. If I kill it, I *can* defeat it! I *will* defeat it! If only she had her sword, her clean silver sword. She remembered coldly Torc's stubborn thought, *Do not kill it, sister! If it dies, you cannot defeat it!* But I will defeat it! She shot without waiting or thinking, pinned her arrow through the side into the table with one swift act that released all her fear, that made her predatory again and aggressive. She watched the wraith squirm, heard its scream, thin and faint like a pinioned rabbit; the arrow was deep, it would not loose itself. The wraith struggled against the table, continued to scream, its blood flowing onto the stone floor as it wrenched ineffectually against her arrow. Quickly she ripped the blanket from the bed into strips. She would tie the creature and leave it. If it died of thirst and hunger and loss of blood, she would be well away, where it could not claim her body.

Yet still she was loathe to touch it. If she touched it, would it possess her? Come into her body through her touch and destroy her? She went sick at the thought of handling it, yet knew she must touch it, must tie it, and more: knew

61

she must search for the runestone among the folds of its clothing.

Did it have the stone? What had happened when Ram fell? She could only see in her memory HaGlard with his sword drawn, then the wraith close and attentive. Think of the stone, Skeelie! Find the stone! Had the wraith snatched it up? She tried to touch some sense of that moment from its mind; but the creature shielded and she could see nothing. She stared at it with repulsion and then with resolution. At last she began to tie it, holding her breath against its stench. It was less like a man than a corpse was. Parody of a man. Parody of death. She tied its hands tightly, then twitched a fold of cape aside and felt along the wraith's body, drew away quickly, sickened. It did not speak, seemed to have lost all desire to speak. Never had she felt such disgust for anything, not even for the dark Seers of Pelli.

At last she forced herself to search its clothing: the folds of cloth, the pockets, and inside the small, once-elegant boots. She found nothing, and turned away retching. The room seemed very close, dank and fetid. Her senses seemed awry, dull and confused, as if something had twisted and warped them. She had to get out of this place, would turn to emptiness if she stayed. She could not bring herself to search further, to examine its body. Grabbing up her pack and bow, she fled the house, bolting the door behind her, jamming the rusted lock through the bolt with relief.

She stood a moment trying to collect herself and put down the sickness, knowing she should go back to search further but unable to do so.

She wandered across a small patch of ground that must once have been Gredillon's garden, confused and uncertain, not knowing what to do. An ancient zayn tree stood tall and sheltering. Ram had spoken of a young zayn tree standing near the house when he was small. There should be a grave nearby, of the small boy with red-dyed hair who had been disguised as Ram and buried here to deceive HarThass in his search for Ram. She found only an indentation in the earth that might have been a grave, sunken in. The marker would long since have rotted. She felt there was a body here, felt the sense of bones, of pale dust, said a short prayer for that unknown child who had helped Ram to live. Standing beneath the zayn tree, staring up at the mountain, she could almost see young Ram running there, surrounded by foxes. The sense of him in this place was so very strong; the sense of his learning years, the sense of his reaching out to mysteries still beyond him, to skills he meant, stubbornly, to make his own.

Gone, now, that childhood. Gone into Time. And yet it would be a part of Ram always. A part she would hold dear to her.

She turned at last, paused before the bolted door, sensed the wraith with distaste, then headed down the trail that would lead to the city of Zandour, walking fast, wanting now only to put space between herself and that dark shadow. As she walked she suddenly remembered Torc, felt fear for the great wolf. Torc had followed the wraith and the Herebians. Why, then, was she not at Tala-charen? Why had she not killed the Herebians as she had meant to do, then dispose of the wraith? What had happened to her?

But Ram had been there; Torc could not have killed the wraith while it could enter Ram's body. Still, she would have attacked the Herebians, helped Ram. Skeelie's pace slowed with her concern for the golden bitch wolf. She stood staring off down the mountain, wondering, worrying.

HIGH UP TALA-CHAREN, Torc lay looking down the cliff to where Ram stood over the two dead Herebian raiders. Her strength was at low ebb, her body light and weak with loss of blood. The painful arrow in her side prevented her from lying out flat in any semblance of comfort. She must go down to Ram now, he was alone. She rose and started down to him.

But the short journey over rocks, which she should have leaped in moments, was slow and painful, and when at last she came down onto the foot of the mountain, she was nearly too weak to go further. She had not spoken to Ram in her mind, but rather had listened, touching his remorse and fury that the wraith had gone, his worry over Skeelie. His anger at the disappearance of the runestone. His ever-present sadness and yearning for the girl called Telien.

When she reached level ground, she skirted the four horses with sense blocking, so as not to frighten them away, and went to stand beside Ram. He was so preoccupied, standing unheeding over the dead Herebians, that he did not see or sense her. She lay down behind him, watching him, knowing she could be patient for a while longer.

Ram kicked with idle anger at the nearest Herebian arm, pushed the body over with his toe. He knew he should strip the corpses of valuables. There could be jewels, money, things he might well need. He knelt at last and turned one of the bodies so he could feel into its pockets. And as he turned it, he saw a glint of silver beneath its shoulder. He held the body up and stared at the silver handle.

Then he drew Skeelie's sword out of the blood and dust. Skeelie's sword! He crouched there holding it, trying to fathom how it had gotten there and could sense nothing. How could Skeelie's sword be here? How could it have been taken from her, except in death? Only a moment before, he had sensed that Skeelie lived, that the wraith had tracked her through Time. He slipped her sword into his belt, turned, and saw the golden bitch wolf lying awkwardly behind him, the arrow sticking out, her thick coat matted with dried blood.

He knelt, took her face in his hands, tipped water into her parched mouth. He tried to make her more comfortable, then quickly made a fire, sick at the thought of what he must do. He must cut the arrow out, and it was deep. He would need herbs, birdmoss for the healing. Great Eresu, he wished Skeelie were there. The look in the wolf's golden eyes told him she would be patient, that she trusted him.

Yet he drew the wolf bell from his tunic and held it a moment. It gave him power; perhaps it would give her strength. Perhaps it could help him to numb the pain of the cutting.

# Part Two

*The Black Lake*

*The tale of NilokEm is evil and dark and leaves questions unanswered and actions unaccounted for. It is clear that that dark Seer alone escaped the slaughter at the Castle of Hape, escaped from Ramad and from the Seers of Carriol. It is said he hid from battle in the deep woods surrounding the castle, and then, the battle done and the castle burned, he rode at last into Farr. It is told that he remained hidden in Farr until talk of the victory at Hape died away, then came from seclusion to build himself a villa with riches gained from evil magic and cruel trading, an elegant villa in the north of Farr, near to where the river Owdneet comes down. And there, too, he constructed the city that later was named Dal. Folk say that NilokEm used dark magic indeed to find a woman that suited him; that he brought her by magic to Farr. Sure it is he bedded her, for she bore him a Seeing son. But no one knows what became of her, for she was not heard of again, once the son was born. Some whispered that NilokEm destroyed her in a fit of rage. Some said that the day his son was born NilokEm became the possessor of a shard of the runestone of Eresu. And there are tales of a battle in the dark wood to the south of Dal, a battle where warriors appeared from out the stuff of thin air to defeat NilokEm. Some say that one of those warriors bore a strong resemblance to NilokEm, though NilokEm had no kin, only his small son for whom the city Dal was built and named.*

*It is sworn by some that Ramad, himself, came out of nowhere to fight against the Seer of darkness, and that the great wolves fought beside him; and that Ramad killed the dark Seer. We of Carriol know not the truth of this, for Ram has not returned to us. We can only pray that his life, wherever he moves, has been as he would will it to be.*

From *The Journal of Tayba of Carriol*, written seventeen years after the battle at the Castle of Hape.

# Chapter Five

SKEELIE MOVED QUICKLY down the mountain. The dropping
sun, a sharp slash of yellow, blurred her view of the trail
and of the city below. Then, as she rounded another curve,
the sun was hidden, leaving only a line of yellow fire along
the edge of the mountain. Ahead of her another trail came
winding down in shadow, little more than an animal trail.
That trail beckoned her, so she turned at once upon it and
began to climb, touched with a spark of excitement, then
of promise. She climbed quickly, never doubting that she
must, scrambling over loose scree and in between close-set
boulders; at the top of a mountain cliff, she stopped surprised, to stare out upon a vast flat plain. Smooth sand,
black and fine as silk, glinting in the falling sun, stretched
away to a line of misty peaks that formed the jagged edge
of the mountain. She was nearly at the top of Scar Mountain,
where its ancient crown had been eaten away by wind and
rain and time to form this dark, silken desert, unmarked by
the print of animal or bird. To her left, at some distance,
gleamed a lake blacker than the sand. She made her way
toward it.

The sense of Ram's childhood still clung around her, the
aura of the dust-wreathed stone house and the ancient garden. A sense of Ram's destiny grew stronger now. She
looked back only once, was surprised by the line of her own
footprints across the silken black sand. How long would
that lonely, alien trail mark this place before the mountain's
winds smoothed it away? When she reached the lake, she
stood looking down at the clear water over black sand and
stones, feeling unaccountably afraid. Then she felt the lake
pulling at her, and knew, suddenly, a strong, terrifying
desire to enter it.

She was not sure when first she was aware of something

stirring around her, of shadows moving subtly across the plain as the shadow of a bird might wing across earth, light and quick, and gone. Did she hear the echo of some sound long vanished? She shivered, and the very air seemed to shift, but when she looked directly anywhere, all was still as before. Yet there was movement at the edges of her vision, movement within her senses, as if she were becoming a part of the fleeting shadows. She knew she must make some decision or she would indeed become a part of those shadows. This time she must choose her own direction or be swept into the meaningless shadows of Time; swept perhaps generations from Ram. She felt so close to him, felt that the thread of his life, picked up like a silken strand there in Gredillon's house, was leading her. She dared not let it slip away. She stared at the black water and knew what she must do and did not know why, made no sense of it. The water pulled at her, some need was reaching out from beyond it and she could not resist.

She argued with herself for some time. The lake stretched away beyond low hills so she could not see the end of it. Could not see down into its depths beyond the first dark rocks and sand. It would be insanity to swim out into that black, concealing water. What did she imagine she would gain by drowning herself in a pool of black water on top of a mountain in a time she could not identify, and where no one would know she was dead, or care? She stared at the black water defiantly. But she knew she was going to do it and began at last to pull off her boots. Then she stood idle for some time deciding about her clothes. It would be foolish beyond measure to go into unknown water fully dressed, to be made helpless by heavy, wet leathers. Yet the thought of removing her protecting garments was worse.

She undressed at last down to her shift and strapped her scabbard of arrows across her naked shoulders, slung on her bow. The water, as she stepped in, was so cold it made an aching, stifling pain in her legs. Surely she had gone mad. She was soon over her head and swimming strongly; trying in desperation to control her panic. With each stroke, as her face went under water, she opened her eyes to stare about her in fear, but could see only dim shadows. Then, suddenly, when she looked up, it was dark. She was swimming through the night, stars overhead and Ere's twin moons hanging low over the water, nearly full, reflecting like a second pair of eyes in the black water. There was no sign of land. Some distance ahead, a black tower rose up out of the water, a tall, unlighted tower, silhouetted against the stars. She swallowed, swam toward it, filled with fear.

When she reached the tower she began to circle it, swimming slowly, looking up. It reared above her like some ancient monster risen from unknown depths, hoary with water weed or with some vine that clung to its sides. At one place, high above her head, she could make out a protrusion like a thick door. When she thought she had circled the tower, she grabbed a handful of vines, tugged at them, found them strong, and began to climb, still following that instinctive Seer's sense of inevitability; and following, too, the only way of escape from the icy water. She climbed until she was out of breath, then clung there shivering. Now she could see the black shapes of hills against the starry sky. There was no sound from within the tower. She pulled herself higher, came to a tiny window and stared in, could see a glint of white, but nothing more. She climbed again, half-naked, cold, wishing for her clothes, her lantern, her sword. Wishing herself home in Carriol, warm and safe in her bed.

She could see high above her a tiny balcony, hardly more than a ledge. By the time she reached it she was warmer, and her shift had begun to dry. She pulled herself up onto it and found she was facing a little barred window. When the wind hit her, she felt cold again. She huddled on the ledge and peered through the bars into the dim stone room. She could see nothing at first but a window directly across from her, where stars shone, a similar window to her left and another to her right. Four windows spaced equally around the circular room. Then she began to make out the room itself. A cot, a chest, a small table, a stool. There was a darker shadow across the cot, like a sleeping figure. As the moons rose higher, she could see the cot better. Yes, someone slept there, long pale hair spilling across the cover.

The figure sighed and stirred, so her face was caught in moonlight. Skeelie's emotions pitched, her fists so tight around the bars her knuckles went white. *Telien? Was it Telien?* Without meaning to, she breathed the name, harsh against the night's silence.

The girl twisted up suddenly, with drawn breath, raised up to face the window; "Who spoke—who?" Slowly she put one bare foot from under the blankets onto the stone floor, then the other foot, almost as if she moved in a dream. She seemed unafraid—or perhaps beyond fear. She came hesitantly toward the window, peering against the faint moonlight. Then she caught her breath. "There is someone! I thought it was a dream. How . . .?" She stared at Skeelie, then reached out through the bars in a frenzy. "How did you . . .? Why, I *know* you! I remember! Skeelie? Is it Skeelie?" Telien knelt on the sill clutching Skeelie close, pulling her into the bars with more strength than one would think she possessed, pressing her face against Skeelie through the bars in an agony of need for warmth, for human contact. Skeelie touched the cold, thin cheek, felt deep hollows where there had been none. She held Telien against her through the bars for a long time while Telien cried silently, shivering. When Telien raised her face at last, the moonlight caught across little lines around her mouth and on her brow. Her hair was no longer golden, but as pale a color as the moons. Skeelie shuddered. How long had Telien been in this place? Why was she here? The girl's confusion, her trembling emotion blurred any sense Skeelie might have taken from her, any answers she might have found.

At last Telien raised her face and stared at Skeelie's near nakedness as if she had just perceived it. Then she rose and drew her blanket from the bed, thrusting it through the bars in a gesture that touched Skeelie terribly.

They had been close once, when Telien was first lost in Time and had cried out to her in spirit, had, in her tumbling frantic flight through ages, needed Skeelie badly. "I wished for you, Skeelie. For a long time after I could no longer feel you in my thoughts, I wished you would come back. But you never did. After a while I stopped wishing."

"I could not. It—the power faded. How long has it been for you, Telien? How many years?" It was only days since Skeelie had left the caves of Owdneet, but surely Telien was years older. She could not understand the warping of Time.

"I don't know how long. My—my baby was born four years after the battle at the Castle of Hape. I have been here nearly since then. I have lost count of years."

"Your—baby?" Skeelie's voice trembled. Whose baby? Ram's baby?

"My baby..." Telien's eyes were dark and huge with her sadness. "I don't want Ram ever to learn of my baby. I—could not face Ramad now. My baby is the child of the dark Seer, Skeelie. The child of NilokEm, who escaped from the battle at the Castle of Hape. My child—my child has the blood of the dark Seers.

"Ni-NilokEm brought me to him out of Time, I do not know how. I was suddenly standing in the garden of his villa. He...I bore NilokEm's child, and then—then my baby was taken from me."

"How long ago was that?"

"I don't know. It was winter when NilokEm locked me here. I think—perhaps four more winters have passed since then. Four winters. It is fall now, I can see color changing on the hills. I lived in his villa for more than a year. Six— six years, then, since I first stood in the garden of NilokEm's villa, terrified of him."

Six years. Skeelie's head spun. How could the number

of days each had lived since they left their own time be different? Six years for Telien, a matter of days for herself.

"Six years since Ramad held me on that windswept mountain. Six years since the huge trees turned suddenly to small saplings, and then we were torn apart. I was alone, Ram was gone in that dark, terrible storm of Time. I have tried not to remember. When that wild storm stopped and all was still, I was in an elegant courtyard, and a man stood watching me, a tall, thin man, stooped, with pale skin and thin dark hair. He terrified me, his look—I knew he was a Seer. I was so afraid of him, I turned to run and saw the gates were bolted with great iron locks. I turned again and would have run through the rooms where a side door opened, but he grabbed me and held me, and . . .

"He—he knew my name without my telling him. He took me to wife." She turned her face away. "I hoped Ram would come, would find me. I was kept locked inside or, if I was let to go about the grounds, I was guarded. I tried to make friends with the guards, hoping they would help me. I had nothing to bribe them with. They were not friendly, they were afraid of NilokEm. I tried to slip back into Time, but I did not know how. I carry the starfire still, but I do not know how to use it. It confuses and upsets me. I have no Seer's powers. I have never known what its power was, but I kept it hidden from NilokEm. I thought sometimes he sensed its power but didn't know what he sensed. I was a prisoner, more confined than when I was watched so constantly in my father's village. I have never understood why NilokEm wanted me, why he called me out of Time. I would not want to see Ram now. But . . . Is Ram safe?"

"He is safe. Somewhere . . ."

"If he knew I had lain with a dark Seer, that I bore that Seer's child . . . When—when NilokEm knew I was with child, he locked me in my room so I could not run away. He kept me there until Dal was born, kept us locked in afterward with a nurse, a mute woman.

"When Dal was weaned, NilokEm took him away from

me. He said my baby would be raised in the villa, and he had me brought here to this tower and locked in. A servant brings me food once a week."

"But why—why does he hate you so? And if he hates you, why does he keep you alive? He could have—"

"Because of the runestone."

Skeelie stared at her. "The runestone you brought out of Tala-charen," she said slowly.

"NilokEm is convinced that I have it, that he can sense its power. But I don't, Skeelie. It is lost. I don't know where. I can't remember where. After that moment on Tala-charen, I was so tired, so confused. I can't remember what happened to it. There was darkness. I can remember sleeping, and then afterward it was gone. But I remember something, Skeelie. I remember clearly that on Tala-charen, at the moment of the splitting of the stone, I saw NilokEm."

"NilokEm? I don't—at the moment of the splitting?"

"He was there, in Tala-charen. Holding a shard of the stone in his cupped hands, hunkering over it, and then gone, faded just as I faded.

"Skeelie, NilokEm possesses a shard of the runestone of Eresu.

"When I first stood in his villa, I knew I had seen him but I could never remember where. Then, just after Dal was born, NilokEm was standing in my room looking down at Dal, and suddenly he disappeared.

"He appeared again in a moment, holding the runestone in his cupped hands, staring at it with amazement, his cheeks flaming red the way he gets when he is terribly excited, eager for something. He . . . I was so tired, dizzy, and confused. I couldn't believe he held a shard of the runestone. I couldn't understand what had happened, not then. I only knew he had come into the birthing room wanting to see *his* heir, then disappeared, then appeared again. When he— when he returned, he stared at me almost with wonder, forgot himself, he was so excited at having the stone. But he had seen me there on Tala-charen, and soon his look turned to terrible fury. I didn't understand what he was saying. He kept shouting. 'That is the secret you harbor! That is the secret!' over and over. He stared at me with terrible hatred. I pulled Dal close and thought he would kill us both. He said, 'That is the power I felt in you! That is why I chose you, because the power of the runestone is on you! You carry a runestone of Eresu! *You* were there on Tala-charen!' He was clutching the runestone in his hand; he held it up flashing green in the lamplight and shouted, 'This one is *my* stone! But *you* carry a shard of the runestone, and I will have it!' He didn't even notice his son. He was . . . he terrified me."

Skeelie held Telien against her, the bars hurting them. The wind came cold; the steel bars were cold as ice.

"He wouldn't believe I didn't have the stone, that I have no Seer's powers. I told him over and over I had no power, that I had lost the stone, and truly, I don't know where it is. He beat me, he took Dal from me and knocked me down. Took . . . took Dal away . . ." Her tears caught light, trickling. "But then Dal would not nurse another, they could not find a wetnurse he would take, so NilokEm had him sent back to me. He swore that when Dal was weaned he would lock me in this tower and leave me here until I told him where the stone is or until I died. But I cannot remember where, I cannot! He beat me over and over. I don't know why he didn't kill me, except he truly believes that one day I will tell him. He wants two runestones; he wants them all. His greed for power—"

"But where . . . ?"

"I do not know where. It is lost somewhere in Time. All of that is confusion to me now, is only a dark dream that comes sometimes so I wake screaming. A churning dream, everything flowing and warping together, one voice drowning another. I can make nothing come clear, Skeelie. I think there is darkness around the stone. I am almost able to remember sometimes, then it is gone. A woman cries out, horses come thundering, there is blood, all so mixed-up, so . . ." She was weeping again, silently, into her hands.

Skeelie pulled her close. They clung so, in silence, warming each other, the bars pressing between them, Skeelie knowing Telien's pain and fear and confusion and not understanding how to help her. Skeelie anticipating Ram's terrible hurt when he learned at last that Telien had borne the son of NilokEm.

She felt awe of the power with which the stone shaped the lives it had touched. How different their lives would be if none of them had ever held the runestone. Why had each of them been drawn to it? And how?

Why, for that matter, was the wraith drawn to it? Had the wraith, too, touched the runestone at some distant time and been ever after drawn greedily back to it?

Had the runestone, then, as much power to offer those of evil as it had to those who battled evil? But of course it did, the very splitting of the stone had come from the violent battling between forces of the light and the dark so evenly balanced, so cataclysmic, that they tore asunder all Time for one blinding instant.

And because he sensed the aura of the stone around Telien, NilokEm had brought her to this time to breed into his heir the power he had thought she held. Skeelie remembered suddenly, startled, what old Gravan had said. The goatherd's voice echoed like a shout in her mind. *Many think NilokEm died, lady, by the hand of Ramad of wolves.* His words pounded over and over. *By the hand of Ramad. By the hand of Ramad.*

"Telien, where is NilokEm?"

"In the villa, I suppose. He never comes here. Skeelie, I felt so helpless, moving through Time I don't know how far, then being pulled back so close to our own time, but unable to reach our time. When I found myself in NilokEm's garden, it was only three years after the battle of the Castle of Hape. But I could not reach that time. I could not reach Ram . . ."

Skeelie remained silent. Three years—and six more years had passed since Telien stood in that garden. Nine years... Old Gravan's words were like a shout in her head. *Some say NilokEm died, lady, by the hand of Ramad— Ramad returned nine years after the battle of the Castle of Hape and killed the last dark Seer.*

*This* year, *this* time, was nine years after the fall of the Castle of Hape. Skeelie wanted to say, *Ram will kill him, Ram will kill NilokEm.* She stared at Telien, a dozen emotions, a dozen thoughts assailing her, and she could not say it; but a thought like ice gripped her: Ram would kill NilokEm if nothing happened, if Time did not warp into a new and unpredicted pattern.

What power might NilokEm hold over Ram with the runestone he held, if Ram did not also carry a shard of the jade? Power enough to change a prediction? And in the meantime, before that prediction came to pass—if it came to pass—what evil deeds would NilokEm accomplish, using the runestone of Eresu?

At least, if Ram were to be cast into this time to battle NilokEm, he need not find Telien captive. He could find her safe, free of this dark tower. Skeelie clung to the bars, the cold wind biting at her, and tried to form some plan. Telien leaned against her nearly asleep, sighing deep inside herself as if her spirit felt quite safe now that Skeelie was there. When Skeelie moved, to stare down the side of the tower, Telien woke suddenly and clung fast to her, "You aren't going away? I thought..."

"I am right here. Where would I go? Telien—how do they bring food to you?"

"There is a drawbridge on the other side. I can see it when they let it down. I can go down there into the lower chamber, to empty my chamber pot. Down past the cells with the bones of men in them. The messenger leaves food down there for me. I can hear him let the bridge down, then hear him walking across it. The hooves of his horse make a hollow sound. I can hear the lock to the inner door rattle, then it opens. I know every movement by the sound. He shouts and leaves the food and goes away again. He has never spoken to me, except for that brutal shout. I wait on the narrow stone stair until he is gone. I always hear him coming and know it is another week.

Skeelie felt sick. She turned away to examine the narrow balcony, though she already knew it ended abruptly and there was no way to get around the tower to the other side except to swim, or to climb along the vines. The top of the tower was high above, and she could see, leaning out, that the vines ended far short of it. She stared below her again. "I saw a small window climbing up here. It was barred. Are there others?"

"There are six. All little, and all barred. You can see them in the lower cells. I tried to dig the bars away in many places, but..."

Skeelie saw where Telien had dug into the dragon-bone mortar and had a sudden quick image of Telien's spoon, ragged and bent from digging. Who knew how deep the bars were set into the mortar. She shook one, then another, then dug with the tip of an arrow. The mortar was nearly as hard as rock. At last she settled her scabbard and bow more comfortably across her shoulders and felt down with her bare toes to find a foothold in the vine. "I will try to reach the drawbridge," she said shortly. The idea of climbing again above the dark water did not enchant her. Telien touched her shoulder, wanting her to stay. Skeelie wriggled her foot into the vines, reached farther with her other foot, swung out, ignoring Telien's need. The girl began to talk rapidly, as if to keep Skeelie there, though Skeelie was already away. Skeelie wished she would be still. "The vine will hold you, Skeelie. It is thick on the banks of the lake, you'll see when it is morning. It grows inside the cells, lower down. Where it was not cut away, it grows right over the white bones of dead men—"

"Telien, take your blanket and go around to the next window. Tie it to the bars, and tie another on if you have it. Find a stick, something to push the blanket to me if I tell you, if the vine grows thin." Anything to keep Telien occupied. Skeelie gripped the vine harder, swung away to her left, jolting the breath out of herself, clung there cold and fearful, gripping vine with her toes. Great Eresu, she wished she were home. She swung on around, reaching and clutching, until at last she saw the blanket hanging just ahead. Above, Telien's white fingers gripped around it where she had reached out through the bars. "You can move the blanket on, I'm all right this far." The blanket jiggled, then made its way upward until the end of it slid over the ledge. Skeelie worked herself on around, feeling out blindly, gripping, clinging, not wanting to look down at the far black water.

She came to the blanket again, feeling as if she might be destined to repeat this action forever, to look up innumerable times to see Telien's white face above her. She pulled herself on around the tower, came to the blanket a third time and, when she looked down, could see a thin silver line crossing over the dark lake, crossing to the shore. A rope? She could see the vine crowding along the shore in thick clumps as if it had climbed over itself again and again reaching for the sky. She made her way downward until she came to the rope where it was fastened into the stone wall of the tower beside a tall slab of wood like a huge door: the wooden drawbridge pulled up against the wall of the tower.

She felt among the vines until she had located the pulley system, then began to haul on the rope. It was awkward, holding herself to the vine with one hand and pulling with the other. But at last the drawbridge began to lower toward the far bank. She clung, resting finally, as its own weight pulled it on down. And it was then, as she rested, that the sense of men drawing near made itself heard in her mind. She clung there cold and aching, very tired, knowing that riders approached. Herebian warriors. And a dark Seer among them.

And did something else move with them? A shadow darker even than NilokEm? A shadow that was death itself, come there seeking? Did it follow NilokEm's runestone?

She saw clearly for a moment, in a cold vision, dark, thin NilokEm, heavy-robed against the night air, riding across open meadows with three dozen warriors at his side, riding hard and silently and less than an hour away. They had warning of her: NilokEm knew she was at the tower.

And then she sensed another rider moving through the wood. Her heart raised with hope. A friend? But as she clung shivering and feeling out to him, she knew he was not a friend.

This was the regular messenger, bringing Telien's food, sent out before Skeelie came to the tower, before NilokEm was aware of her there.

The messenger would bring the food and leave. NilokEm and his band meant to stay long enough to see that Skeelie would never leave the tower alive, for they knew her for a Seer. But the wraith intended that she live. Following its own purposes, suffering from festering wounds in a sick body, it sought like a beast of prey for a new body. She felt that its will and its power had strengthened. Why? *Did* it carry the runestone that should have been Ram's and draw strength somehow from the jade? A tremor touched her. Her hands shook. The wraith meant to find a new home for the bodiless evil that was all that remained of a thing once human. Its intent, cold seeking filled her. It meant that she would leave the tower alive and soulless, empty inside herself save for its own presence. But why her? Why not NilokEm? NilokEm, too, was a Seer. Did the fact that he carried a runestone make him too powerful for the wraith to overcome? Or did she, by her friendship with Ram, who had held the stone at its splitting and who surely was destined to join together that stone, if ever that should happen, did she through that friendship present some even more compelling scent to the weasellike wraith?

# Chapter Six

TORC LAY before Ram's fire, her shoulder bandaged, her eyes closed in a deep, dreamless sleep. Ram crouched on the other side of the fire, exhausted, his hands stained with her blood, the Herebian arrow lying at his feet. The strength of his mind-power over the bitch wolf, giving her blessed sleep, was all that had enabled him to cut so deeply into her shoulder. He kept the shadows heavy on her mind, now, for she needed rest. He wished they could both sleep, but was afraid that without the spell she would wake and the pain would be too great.

He kept her so for several days, her mind shadowed into sleep against the pain, her wound packed with birdmoss, which he gathered along the banks of a small, fast stream. He hunted for the two of them, let her wake sufficiently to eat. Took his own rest in short, fitful periods. He had hobbled the four Herebian mounts, though he meant to turn all but one loose when at last Torc was able to travel. If he did not suddenly disappear from this meadow, leaving the hobbled horses, and also leaving Torc to travel alone.

By the fifth day she was well enough so she needed no more spells for sleeping. Ram slept the night around and sat beside her the next morning much improved, roasting rock hares over the coals. He had stripped the Herebians of their valuables and buried the bodies beneath stones at the base of the mountain, wishing he were burying the wraith with its dark soul intact in it. Skeelie's sword hung from his belt. The bitch wolf watched him now, across a fire gone nearly invisible in the bright morning sun. Her golden eyes were steady, but her thoughts were drawn away in some private vision that she did not share with him. He reached to lay more wood on the coals, and suddenly her thought hit him quick and surprising, jarring him so he dropped the wood, making the fire spark wildly. "What, Torc?" He stared at the golden bitch, her head lifted regally, watching him. "What did you say, Torc?"

*Why is the wraith linked to Anchorstar?* She repeated. *Do you not feel it, Ramad? I see it as if in some future time; I see the wraith feeding on the pain of young Seers still as death. All in the future, Ramad. And Anchorstar is there.*

Ram turned the rock hares with a shaking hand. Fat dripped down to make the flames leap anew, smoke twisting against sunlight. "Why is he there, Torc? As victim of the wraith? Or—as accomplice?"

*As victim, Ramad. Sleeping, drugged, as close to death as those young Seers.*

He breathed easier. He would not have liked betrayal by Anchorstar, would not have liked betrayal by his own senses in trusting Anchorstar so implicitly. He took from his pocket the three starfires that Anchorstar had given him and held them near the flame, watched them catch dark green streaks within, then turn to amber once more. He looked up at Torc, squinting against the sun. "Is your vision a true one?"

*As true as any vision of future time can be, Ramad of wolves.*

"If it is so, then Anchorstar will need all the power he can muster." He touched the starfires. "I do not see what the future holds for Anchorstar, but I know he suffers deep within. I have never plumbed those depths, nor do I understand Anchorstar well. I hope that by giving me the starfires he has not weakened his own power. If I could help him, there in that future time, I would do so. I would give back the starfires if it would help."

*The starfires are a treasured gift, Ramad.*

"Though they have little power, I think, other than to move through Time. Strange stones, Torc. I cannot guide my fall through Time by them, yet I feel their power in the very warping that Time makes. Sometimes I feel, like Anchorstar, that I should cast them away."

*I would not, Ramad. You could do great harm by that.*

*All is linked. All. The starfires, Anchorstar, the wraith, Skeelie—more than you know. Telien is linked to all of it.*

"Linked—how? You have taken a prophetic turn, Torc."

*I do not know how. I only see it. Lying here half in fog, mesmerized by your Seer's skills, Ramad—visions came. Sweeping senses like the gray fog swirling up, and then gone. No reason to it. Only the sense of it, a sense of purposeful linking, of creatures touching across Time, meeting across Time in some meaning and purpose I do not comprehend. A sense of your lady, Telien, linked to all of it.*

Telien. He saw her face in a memory filled with pain, her green eyes clear as the sea. Was it memory or vision? His emotions and his longing for Telien were so raw he could never be sure. Perhaps memory and vision muddled together; but now he sensed her in a time long past. He was very sure of that suddenly. Had she returned to their own time? He saw danger around her, saw cruelty touch her, a vision immersed in darkness, filled with agony. He reached out his hand involuntarily, and burned his fingers in the fire, then sat staring morosely at the flame. Torc watched him in silence.

When he looked up at last, he was tense with purpose. "I must be with her, Torc. Somehow, I must. She is in need. When I try to reach out, nothing comes. The starfires do not help me, never help me. But I know she is in need."

And there was another vision that touched him, puzzling him, seemed to be linked to Telien, though he could not understand how. A young Seer reached out to him in dreams, a young redheaded man with clear blue eyes. And something, perhaps the turn of his cheek, so like Telien that Ram could not forget his face; a young Seer reaching out of Time to speak to him not in words but with a need that Ram knew he must at last acknowledge. There was surely a linking between them, they were creatures linked across Time somehow. But what was that linking? And how was Telien a part of this? The young Seer seemed to hold in his mind repeated visions of Ram and the wolves fighting beside him; as if he needed Ram, would purposely draw him into another time and yet another battle if he could. As he had been drawn into Macmen's battle. And did that other Seer hold a runestone, just as Macmen had? Ram dared not dream that he did. Yet he sensed a power that the young, untrained Seer seemed to wield with little assurance. Ram knew he must reach out to him, that it was not only Telien he must seek—though it was Telien his seeking spirit longed for. He looked across at Torc. Who was this young Seer who beckoned to him now? Torc watched him in silence, seeing his thoughts with sympathy. And, feeling her kindness, his longing for Fawdref and Rhymannie and their pack came sudden and sharp. "They have not been with me, Torc. Fawdref and Rhymannie were swept away even as I was, into Time. The rest of the pack was not with us, might still be in our own time, I do not know."

*They are not in our time, Ramad. The pack did not return to the mountain after the battle at the Castle of Hape. I was not with the pack when they attacked the castle, I was in the whelping dens, awaiting my cubs.* She paused, then went on. *The pack did not return there. But I know that my mate was killed, battling at the Castle of Hape. He spoke clearly in my mind then. Spoke of private things. They—the band will be with you, Ramad, if they are needed. Call them. Speak to them with the bell. Fawdref is growing old. He needs you, now, as much as you need him.*

HERMETH SAW the enemy driven back, saw his men resting from battle where they had fallen, where tired horses had stopped to blow. Soldiers began to sponge away blood with water from their waterskins, dressing the wounds of their animals before they tended themselves and their brothers. He ached with fatigue, with remorse at the waste of war, stared out across the near-dark remains of what had so recently been farm buildings. milking pens, now only smoking rubble peopled with the corpses of horses and men. Waste, desolation, just as his father before him had known at the hands of the Herebian raiders—at the hands of dark Seers Macmen thought he had destroyed in his last great battle, the year that Hermeth himself was born. Hermeth sighed and considered the desolation before him with some sense of victory, for they had driven the bastards back, had sent a fresh battalion to pursue them on good mounts, to slaughter every Herebian son of . . . He lowered his head suddenly and clenched his eyes closed as another vision swept him. The battlefield disappeared; he saw a wolf again, only one wolf this time. A golden bitch wolf with golden eyes reflecting the light of a campfire. Across from her sat the dark-eyed Seer he saw each time a vision came. He was leaning to turn roasting rock hares, his red hair so bright in the morning sun it seemed to dim the firelight. The wolf wore some sort of poultice on her shoulder. The young Seer wore two swords now, one with a carved silver hilt. The vision faded slowly, firelight and sunlight filtering together until it dazzled his eyes; and the figures were gone.

Why did such visions haunt him? He had never in his life had visions; his Seer's skills had never been strong. These visions were so real he could smell the fire and the roasting rock hares, and feel the cold breeze. Feel sharply his need to speak to that Seer. Surely there was a meaning, surely it was the runestone he carried that made such power in him. But why did it do so now, when it never had before? Did the runestone itself have some mysterious link to that young, dark-eyed Seer?

Hermeth knew his skills had come stronger since his visions began. The conjuring he had laid upon the sheep pastures, to deceive the rabble raiders, had been more than satisfying; that memory still left him with a shock of surprise that he had been capable of such. And his power seemed linked to the other Seer; he felt that they were meant somehow to stand together in battle, though he could not divine the reason. Had that, too, to do with the stone? He felt increasingly that he needed that other Seer in a battle yet to come. He stared into the thickening dark, puzzling. A fitful wind touched his cheek, blowing down from the high deserts that rose above the rim, and he seemed to touch a sudden and desolate sense of space, of eternity, that dizzied him, made him draw back, want human company. He turned away toward the cookfires where his men were tending their wounds, knelt beside a young soldier and took the bandage from his hands, began to wrap the boy's arm. When he looked up at last, the cast of firelight caught his men's faces in a quiet brotherhood that stirred him deeply, the brotherhood of soldiers who knew they might die together, soldiers who fought together fiercely.

Wars had flared, died, moved across the coastal countries like a series of sudden storms, the raiders appearing in one place then disappearing suddenly. Sly, clever bands took shelter in the rough hills and woods, then slipped out to leave families dead and crops and homes destroyed. Slowly then the Herebian bands, provisioned from what they did not destroy and armed anew, drew ever closer to the ruling city of Zandour. So far they had been thwarted in Sangur and Aybil and Farr, or sometimes set one against the other when Hermeth could conjure friction and quarrels through a few trusted men who traveled among the enemy troops. This close, efficient network of spies was the first such in Ere since Carriol had come to power and, after the battle of Hape, sent out small cadres across Ere as protection against the dark Seers rising anew.

Though Carriol herself had changed her ways more than a generation ago and now spent her Seer's powers—so much less without the runestone that Ramad had wielded, countless years back in her history—to hold solid her own borders, protecting those who would come to her for sanctuary, but letting the rest of Ere fend as best it could.

And now the sons of the dark twins, street-bred sons of whores, drew closer upon Zandour in these small, agile bands, easily lost among the hills and woods, impossible to track sometimes, except by Seeing. And Hermeth's small handful of Seers was not omniscient. Seers tire, too. Seers grow weary in war and, grown weary, become uncertain in their skills.

He remembered with satisfaction that time in Aybil, in the curve of the bay nearest to the sunken island of Dogda, when he had laid a vision-trap that brought forty Herebian warriors down upon what they thought were sheep farmers and turned out to be soldiers herding boulders. That was a victory. But his skill of vision-making was uneven, and not often to be relied upon.

He thought of the power that that other Seer must wield. He coveted that power, not for himself, but to win this cursed war; envied the strength of mind he sensed in that Seer, was drawn to that young man who could command the great wolves and, most likely, command the powers of a runestone with none of his own hesitation. At times the stone would not work for him at all. He would feel a darkness then, a shadow around him; and the runestone would be lifeless in his hands so the visions would not come, let alone any illusion-making.

Then the veil would lift, and visions would come sharply. He would imagine that Seer and a great band of wolves fighting by his side, defeating the street Seers of Pelli. Was that Seer heir to Ramad, who had lived at the time of the Hape? Surely he must carry the wolf bell that had belonged to Ramad, for how else could he wield power over the great wolves? Hermeth scowled, puzzling. He thought of his father and the story of his victory over the dark twins. A mysterious warrior had fought by Macmen's side. A warrior commanding wolves and believed by many in Zandour to have been Ramad of wolves come mysteriously across Time. Macmen's own stories, when Hermeth was small— before Macmen died in Hermeth's sixth year—had named that warrior Ramad. But mustn't he in truth have been the grandson of Ramad, also named Ramad? The stories were garbled and unclear. The original Ramad had battled NilokEm nine years after the battle of the Castle of Hape, nearly ninety years gone in Ere's past.

Hermeth felt overwhelmed with questions. It would make no sense for a vision to come to him of the original Ramad, long dead. Not when he envisioned so clearly that Seer fighting beside him. Could the redheaded Seer of his visions be the son of the second Ramad, son of the Ramad who had fought by Macmen's side? Was this young man drawn to him now by the ties that their two sires had known on the battlefield?

WHEN SHE HAD the drawbridge down, Skeelie found that an arrow was of little use in trying to undo the great iron lock on the door. Only the tip of the blade would go in, and the hasp was long and well set into the wood. It was hard to work by moonlight. She fiddled with the hinges, found one somewhat loose where the wood was softer. The panic of the closely approaching rider made her nervy, and she was fearful of the large band of riders farther off. Carefully, but with trembling hands, she began to dig out the hinge.

She hacked at the wood, dug, carved at it until at last she was able to work her arrow tip under and pry the hinge loose. When it came free, she began working on the lower one, which seemed solid indeed. She listened with growing tension for the galloping messenger, tried to plan what to do, swore at the lower hinge, which was set into the wood as if it had grown there.

She heard him before she had made even a dent in the wood. Exasperated, fearful, she drew back into the shadow of the door, her arrow taut in the bow.

He drew up his horse at the far bank and sat staring across, filled with apprehension, gazing into the shadows of the tower searching for the intruders who had lowered the drawbridge. Could he see her? The angle of the moons left only deep shadow where she stood, but some light came from the star-washed sky. She hardly breathed.

At last, with drawn sword, he urged his horse onto the bridge, approaching slowly and deliberately. The horse's hooves struck hollow echoes. Skeelie knew the horse smelled her, could feel it tensed to shy. She soothed its mind until it calmed and came on quietly. Then when it was nearly on top of her she leaped out, shouting and waving her arms. The good animal screamed in terror and spun, nearly went over backward in its panic, dumped its rider and stepped on his arm as it lost its footing and fought to avoid the lake. It righted itself, then hammered away across the bridge and disappeared into the wood.

The rider half rose, groaning; crouched facing Skeelie, her drawn arrow inches from his face.

"Get up, soldier."

He rose, staring at her with fury.

"Unlock the door. Hurry."

He fumbled with the key, pushed it into the lock with shaking hands, got the door open at last, pushed it to. The cell room was dimly lit where moonlight crept through small cell windows. Barred cells rose all around, tier upon tier, with a winding stairway like a great snake leading up.

"Go in ahead of me. Stand in the center of the room. Where is the food?"

He stood in the moonlight facing her, dropped a leather pouch at his feet.

"Unsling your bow and your arrows and drop them. Your knife. Then step away from them, over by that cell."

The man stared at the cell, then glanced at his knife still in the scabbard. She raised her arrow a quarter inch and drew her bow tauter. He removed the knife and dropped it.

"Now take your leathers off. Take your boots off. Toss them here. And the key."

He stared at her with fury. At last he began to peel off his fighting leathers. She heard the key clink at her feet. When he was stripped to graying undergarments, she nodded toward the cell and he, docile now in his near nakedness, went into it. She gestured, and he pushed the door closed. "You would not leave me, miss. Not to starve, not to die of thirst here . . ."

"There are riders coming. They will set you free. If they find you." Skeelie saw Telien then on the narrow stair that led to the top of the tower. "There is a horse, Telien, go catch it; you are good with horses. Take—take his knife and bow." She thought Telien would be afraid, would refuse. But the thin girl did as she was bid quickly, taking up the weapons and slipping out the door and across the wooden bridge soundlessly in her bare feet.

Skeelie fitted the key to the cell door.

"Miss, don't lock me in here. I was only—I didn't hurt her, I was only bringing her food."

Skeelie locked the door and rattled it, gave the messenger a cold look, pulled on his leathers, all too big for her, rolled up the pants, the sleeves. She put on the boots, but they were impossible. She took them off again and tossed them into a locked cell halfway up the hall. She could see white bones in some of the cells.

She left the tower, locked the door behind her, pocketed the key, and ran noiselessly across the drawbridge. Her heart had begun to pound again, in a panic with the closeness of the riders. She found the rope, pulled the drawbridge up, straining with its weight. Then she stood silent, reaching out to Telien. Yes, there—she ran, her heart like a hammer, toward where Telien held the big Herebian mount on short rein among the black trees. Good girl! She was mounted, gave Skeelie a hand up, and they were off at a gallop across the soft carpet of leaves. "West," Skeelie whispered. "They come, NilokEm comes at us from the north." The moons were dropping down, would be behind the hills soon. Already in the east the sky above the trees was growing gray.

HERMETH'S SOLDIERS pinned one cadre of the rabble invaders against a cliff and slaughtered them, but the main army melted away into the hills, and there hid waiting for dusk. Hermeth sent a rider fast across the hills to bring additional troops from out the sheep fields and farms, to raise a new wave of attack. Then he climbed alone up the high hill beside which his armies were camped, stood staring down across the green valley, cast in shadow now as the sun fell. Far out on the meadows the night patrol circled in silence. Behind him, on the far side of the hill, two sentries stood shielded among boulders watching the darkening plains, and below, his men were building supper fires, tending the wounded, caring for the mounts. An army resting after battle, a scene so often repeated it sickened him. He was sick of fighting, wanted it over with, wanted to see his men marching home freed at last from the Pellian manace, from the Pellian greed for land and riches, freed to live in peace as men were meant to live. His hatred of the rabble Seers burned inside him, a festering hatred of men who could think of nothing but attack and theft and killing. Now, only Farr lay between his troops and Pelli itself. Farr where half the country held allegiance to the dark street rabble. Though the other half would stand with Zandour, if need be.

And there might be need. If he could destroy this army he followed, he could break the back of the Pellian rabble. He felt the sense of the rabble Seers leading them. Only a handful, but strong in their skills; and they wanted the runestone above all else; they lusted for it harder than they lusted to rape and burn and kill.

Alone on the hilltop as evening fell, he tried to reach out across space, across elements he little understood. He needed that other Seer's power to help him now, that Seer who commanded such skill with the wolf bell and would surely wield the power of the runestone better than ever he could himself. He felt sometimes, with the stone he carried, like a child trying to learn speech, and no one to teach him the words. He needed power now against the rabble leaders, for if they were not destroyed soon, perhaps they would grow so strong that Zandour would never be free of them. One handful of greedy street waifs risen to such strength. One handful drawing to them every lusting Herebian raider they could muster and holding them with promises of power.

He slipped the runestone from his tunic, held it so it caught the last light of the vanished sun. This runestone, which their common ancestor had commanded: NilokEm, from whose seed both Hermeth, himself, and the dark street rabble had sprung. He wondered fleetingly who that unnamed woman, his great-grandmother, had been who had borne their common grandfather then disappeared so mysteriously.

He watched night fall around him, watched the supper fires die at the base of the hill and his men roll into their blankets, to sleep exhausted. The guards circled in the thickening dark; then he felt the darkness shift and felt unfamiliar shadows move upon the hill, felt the sense of expectancy that foreshadowed the appearance of a vision, stood staring eagerly into the darkness, clutching the runestone, and felt rather than saw the shadow standing tall with the great wolf beside him. But then the figures were gone again as if they had never been, and the hills curved empty in the deepening night.

At long last Hermeth went down to his men, heavy with disappointment.

RAM SENSED the other's presence, then felt a lulling emptiness as if that other Seer had turned and gone away into shifting shadows. He stood beside Torc, with his hand on her shoulder, where she had risen at the first sense of the vision. They waited, he, tense and expectant, and at last the shadows came strong again, the familiar shifting of earth and sky, and he and Torc stood suddenly upon a hill watching a figure descend to where campfires flickered in the night, where men slept with weapons by their sides, exhausted from battle. He stood looking down the hill, filled with the sense of a meeting imminent, of a power between himself and that receding figure. Why? Did that Seer carry a shard of the runestone? The sense of such power was strong. He saw in his mind the young man's face, the turn of his cheek so like Telien. Pale brows, sandy lashes like

Telien's. But was there another resemblance, too? Or did he only imagine the likeness to Macmen?

Macmen had stood quietly after defeating his twin brothers, holding with reverence the runestone that he had won from them. Macmen—the square face, the square cut to his chin very like this young man. Though Macmen's coloring was darker.

In what time was this hill on which he now stood? In what time did this young man live? Ram sensed a pattern intricate and all powerful, a pattern that seemed woven of the powers of mind and earth, equally awing him. Macmen's son had been born in the year Ram fought beside Macmen. Macmen's son . . .

The sense of that pattern vanished, leaving him taut with desire for the hidden answers it held. He stood watching the redheaded figure moving now among the troops. Torc pressed close to his side. *That is what I felt, Ramad, that sense of a linking, of creatures and powers touching. But wait—there are others with us.* Ram could feel Torc's pleasure, then felt other bodies against his legs, and the great wolves were pushing all around him in wild confusion. He nearly shouted with delight, knelt to embrace them, their wild reality leaping into crazy joy. He hugged Fawdref, felt the great wolf take his hand between killer's teeth, pressing gently. Rhymannie nuzzled him, the wolves pushed at him, nearly toppling him in their delight. He was drowning in a sea of wolves, delirious; huge shaggy bodies pressing and licking with wolfish humor as they bit and pushed and nuzzled.

When he rose at last and glanced down the hill, he saw the figure standing below staring up at them, felt the young Seer's wonder. Then the man climbed quickly, and stood before him at last, caught in silence. The moonlight touched his red hair, his sandy brows and pale lashes, the light, clear depths of his eyes. "I do not know your name. But who else would walk with wolves except the son of the second Ramad?"

"There was only one Ramad. And I am not his son."

"Who, then?"

"I am Ramad."

"You cannot be Ramad; perhaps Ramad's son fought beside my father twenty-three years past, in the summer that I was born. But you cannot be he and surely not Ramad of the wolves."

"I am Ramad. You must take my word. And you are the son of Macmen. You are Hermeth. I remember you as a babe," Ram said, grinning.

Hermeth stared and could not believe. They were of an age, surely. He studied Ram; the smooth cheek, the dark eyes beneath thick red hair. He saw the wolf bell Ram took from his tunic. He felt the sense of Ram's truth. At last he held out his open hand, where the shard of the runestone gleamed. Trusting beyond question, he dropped it into Ram's hand. It lay like a dark slash across Ram's palm, and a drumming of power like thunder shook them. Hermeth's green eyes looked into Ram's dark eyes and laughed. Time grew huge around them. The wolves raised their voices in a wail that chilled the blood and panicked the horses tied in the valley below and woke four battalions of sleeping soldiers, who leaped up drawing weapons, before Hermeth spoke down to them.

At last the soldiers rolled back into their blankets and slept. The sense of the power of the stone calmed. Ram and Hermeth stood staring at one another, both filled with questions, Ram with perhaps even more curiosity than burdened the young ruler of Zandour. This meeting with Hermeth, so long foreshadowed, seemed to open his mind to every puzzling thought he had pushed aside. He felt it as a turning place, though he did not know why or how. Questions came that touched on the core of his being, on the nature of his own power and of the power of the runestone. On the nature of the compromise he must find within himself between his search for Telien and his search for the shards of the runestone.

He looked at Hermeth and felt for an instant he was seeing the shadow of Telien. What was this likeness to Telien that made him think such thoughts. What was he trying to unravel, to imagine? He had a sense of Time curving in on itself, touching itself at its own beginnings, and this confused and upset him.

Then he put such thoughts aside, smiled at Hermeth, and they descended the hill thinking of a hot brew. Ram did not notice until later that Torc was no longer with them, no longer among the wolves that crowded around him down the hill; did not sense the pattern of unseen forces, and the will of Torc herself, that twisted her away into another time, far distant.

# Chapter Seven

BY MORNING, fresh Zandourian soldiers had arrived, and two heavily armed battalions of Aybilian soldiers as well, joining Hermeth on good horses, as eager to destroy the rabble raiders as was the Zandourian band. Ram, mounted on a fast Zandourian stallion, carried the runestone now. He felt out into the hills of Aybil with strengthened senses and spotted five bands hidden. Hermeth sent silent riders, with wolves among them like shadows to track the hidden killers, while his main army moved on through Aybil's valleys, toward Farr. The river Owdneet would be on their left soon, for they were headed toward a point just south of the Farrian city of Dal. There were scattered groups of raiders in Farr, and Hermeth meant to destroy them all before he rode on Pelli.

For three days they fought skirmishes down across Aybil, the wolves and scouts routing out raiders' camps, killing so many that the rabble fought back with waning spirit, fought fearfully, then at last turned tail and fled before Hermeth's raging troops. Hermeth's men grinned with bloodstained faces, tired and hungry and not caring, preferring to fight, for victory lay close at hand.

But if men can forget rest in the rising tide of winning, horses cannot. At last, as Hermeth's troops crossed into Farr somewhat south of Dal, Hermeth knew they must halt, at least by midday, and rest the mounts and care for them.

There lay close ahead a thick wood that would give them cover. Hermeth headed for it, but Ram stopped him, uneasy. He sat his tired horse, trying to sort out the unease he felt, then at last chose scouts among the wolves and called a dozen troops to ride with them.

But all returned from the wood, after a thorough search, with nothing to report. *It is quiet there, Ramad,* said the gray wolf who had led them. *There is nothing to fear. And yet . . .*

"And yet, Gartthed? What is it?"

*I don't know. Perhaps nothing. It is peaceful there—perhaps too peaceful. There is a tower there, a dark, ruined tower ages old. It is too peaceful around that tower, too quiet. But perhaps—perhaps I imagine things. There is nothing to alarm, nothing one can sense or see. It smells only of moss and painon bark and woods things. An old, old wood it is, the trees huge and bent.*

IN THE WOOD, the whore-bred Seers stood huddled together in a circle beneath those huge trees, hands joined and fingers linked in a ritual of Pellian cunning as they conjured a mindfog, a false peace and emptiness that hid them all and hid their mounted warriors from Hermeth's Seer-scouts and from the accursed wolves. They had not planned on wolves. Where in Urdd had wolves come from? Near them among the trees, their Farrian and Pellian troops mounted on heavy horses stood silent and invisible by the power of that mind-twisting, heavily armed troops waiting for Hermeth's army. And if the whore-bred Seers felt a power other than their own there, a power in the wood that they could not sort out, they did not pause to question it. Nothing could be so strong as they. The smiled coldly and brought a stronger force yet of unawareness onto Hermeth's approaching army, a mood of simple trust so that Ramad and Hermeth and their men entered into shadow thinking only of rest and a hot meal and a tip of the wineskin to ease the pain of wounds.

SKEELIE AND TELIEN kept the horse to a walk, in order to move as silently as they could through the sparse wood. Dawn had begun to filter between the slim young trees. They rode over soft, damp leaves that muffled sound; but muffled the sound of riders behind them, too. And those riders knew they were there, followed them not by sound but by Seer's skills. "It is growing light, Skeelie. They will be able to see us now."

"It doesn't make much difference," Skeelie said dourly. She began, with more determination than faith, to try to conjure an illusion that might confuse and turn aside NilokEm's troops. If she *could* turn them aside, if she could even begin to deceive that dark Seer. He was no simple Herebian raider, to be so easily deceived as had been the warriors by the lake of fire. He was NilokEm, strong in his dark Seer's powers, strengthened by the shard of the rune-stone he carried. Still she must try; their lives could well depend on such deception. What illusion could turn such a man aside, terrify him? Turn his soldiers back, frighten his horses as she had frightened the messenger's mount? Something—she thought of a trick Ram had used when they were children: A vision of wolves raging in bloodthirsty attack. Oh yes, a vision of wolves might do it.

The vision rose in her mind, great dark wolves snarling and leaping. But could she make NilokEm see them? She began to conjure their shapes from the shadows beneath the trees, to turn and form the shadows; forcing her power into them until she could feel the mount beneath her cringe as the wolves took shadowy form around it. Telien fought to keep the horse from bolting. Skeelie brought wolves huge and leaping out of darkness, felt elation at her own strength, brought wolves stronger still, bolder, drew them close, a sea of snarling killers. Their frightened mount stood motionless now, crouching and shivering, wanting to explode in terror, but its fear gripping it in dumb immobility. Skeelie gave the wolves a rank scent, heightened their snarls; and in one lurching surge sent them streaking to where NilokEm's horses crashed through the wood. She heard horses scream as they reared and spun. Branches shattered. Men cried out, swearing, caught in confusion.

But one wolf did not follow the rest, remained close beside their plunging horse, one wolf golden in the wash of dawn that fell between the slim trees. "Torc! Oh, Torc!"

Skeelie felt the bitch wolf's laughter and went weak with pleasure.

*Hold the image, sister! Do not let it fade!*

She caught her breath, brought the image-wolves into wilder attack among the bolting horses. Their own horse fought Telien, tried to run suddenly. "Pull the horse up, Telien! Pull him up!" Though Telien was doing all she could, sawing its reins and jerking the animal in a circle. Skeelie stared down at Torc, so very glad to see the bitch wolf. *Where did you come from? How . . . ?* The horse continued to spin, fighting Telien. Torc stood still, so as not to alarm it further. *Out of another place, sister, out of another time that . . .* but the shadows were shifting around them, the wood shifting and warping. The light changed suddenly: sun shone bright between thick branches of trees grown huge, ancient. Their horse spun now in terror, nearly fell, then stopped at last to stand trembling again, foam coating its neck. Around them, riders surged closer in a storm of confusion as Skeelie's image-wolves leaped and snarled. Their horse crouched wild-eyed, as if it would throw itself. Skeelie slid off to safety, pulling Telien with her, though Telien tried to cling.

"Don't, Skeelie! It's only frightened, don't . . ." The big mount snorted and reared, pulling Telien off her feet. Skeelie sensed a movement behind her and spun, saw Torc leap for a man who was nearly on top of them, his sword glinting.

*The image, sister! The image!* For the image-wolves had wavered again; Skeelie sent the vision stronger until wolves leaped once more, keening among the panicked raiders. In the confusion their horse turned and ran, the bit hard in his mouth so Telien was dragged at the end of the reins, her heels digging into the soft earth, then was forced to let him go. NilokEm's soldiers and the image-wolves churned in a melee of confusion among ancient trees gnarled and thick beneath a high noon sun, all semblance of a young wood vanished into a time long dead.

And something else was happening in the wood. At the

moment that the slim trees turned ancient, and the sun brightened, other forces were there; dark powers rising at cross-purposes to NilokEm's powers; and other powers, powers of light. Forces clashed and rose, clashed anew.

HERMETH'S TROOPS, come into the wood slowly and quietly and wanting rest, were startled into action suddenly, drew weapons, and spun their horses to face the circle of rabble made suddenly visible, penning them in; rabble that had slipped under cover of mind-fogging into a tight circle around them. Hermeth's men lashed into them and all the violence of Urdd broke loose as, at the same instant, the woods shivered with overlapping images, warping, then the ancient trees came steady again; and another band of soldiers was there among them battling wolves in a confusion even Ram could not sort out. The rabble he and Hermeth had pursued was all around them, but facing strange soldiers now and strange wolves all come out of nowhere, in a senseless tangle. Come out of Time? Or were those other wolves image-wrought? And what were these troops? He slashed at a soldier, fought fiercely but abstractly, trying to make sense of the confusion.

NilokEm's soldiers struck from the saddle at wolves and struck only air. They battled soldiers come out of nowhere, powers come out of nowhere. The dark Seer swore at their sudden fear, at powers gone awry. He brought his own powers down hard and felt them twisted and muted, fought his rearing horse with cruel fury, slashed at a Herebian bearing down on him. Then suddenly he saw ahead of him a flash of pale hair caught in sunlight, and he forgot wolves, forgot the confusion of warriors come out of nowhere, forced bloody spurs into his horse, and rode after Telien with sword drawn. His men, seeing him turn tail, facing wolves they could not kill, facing too many soldiers, jerked their horses and bolted in cold fear—but now again they met wolves, and these animals pulled men from the saddle and took horses down at full run. There was no escape, there was nothing to do but fight.

NilokEm bore down on Telien, then pulled his horse up suddenly as the cold presence of other Seers exploded in his mind; dark Seers behind him. How could that be? Even his hatred of Telien could not hold him. He spun his horse, searching for the rabble Seers among the troops that battled his men, puzzled and furious. There *were* no other dark Seers, not in all of Ere, not even such rabble as these. *He* was the last with such power, until Dal grew to an age to master such skills. But there *were* dark Seers here! Where had such Seers come from? And did he sense Seers of light? He sat his fidgeting horse still as stone, reaching out. And there was something else besides, something even more disturbing—or perhaps opportune. Could he be sensing clearly?

Yes, yes. There was a runestone here, he thought with rising excitement. One of those Seers carried a runestone, he could feel the power of it. His eyes grew dark and slitted with greed as he surveyed the raging battle, sorting, feeling out to find the bearer of that stone.

He did not search out for long, for snarling wolves surrounded him, singled him out, their eyes filling him with terror. A huge, dark dog wolf leaped for his leg as his horse reared, and another went for its throat. He lashed at them from the saddle, flailed with his sword, but they were too quick; his stricken horse twisted and fell, its throat gushing blood. He leaped free, faced a dozen wolves as the battle churned around him. He brought the power of the stone against them, drove them back snarling with pain. But again they advanced, strong-willed against the stone's power, heads lowered. He sought the stone's forces stronger—but he felt nothing suddenly. Nothing. He stared down at the stone, stricken. It lay lifeless and dull in his hand. The wolves paused, watching him, anticipating something. He felt the stone's absence of power with terror. What he felt happening was impossible, incredible.

Was that other stone, carried by one of those Seers, stealing the power from this stone? How could such a thing be?

The wolves stood appraising him, their eyes slitted in eager anticipation that chilled him to the bone. Then suddenly the stone flared burning in his hand so he screamed and dropped it, saw the jade pulsing like fire at his feet.

At the same instant the stone in Ram's hand turned to flame, seared him. He held it, gritting his teeth, did not know what was happening, would not let the stone go. He blew, spat on it. At last it cooled, lay green again in his painfully burned palm. He was aware suddenly of the dark Seer facing him across the battlefield, was locked suddenly as if with bands of steel to that Seer. They stood, Ramad and NilokEm, facing across the melee of battle, two Seers come together, locked together in painful contest for possession of one shard of the runestone of Eresu that lay, in that instant, split in its nature: one stone, handed down from NilokEm to Dal, to the dark twins, taken in battle by Macmen, given to Hermeth, and given then to Ram. It could not exist for long divided. It must draw into itself, become one, and the stronger Seer would draw the stone's strength to himself. Their wills dwarfed the battle that raged as Hermeth's men fought Pellians out of Time and Pellians contemporary.

Sweat streaked Ram's forehead as he forced his power against NilokEm. The dark Seer went ashen, then rallied, began to draw the force of the stone in a surge of desperation. It was then Ram saw Telien leaning half-conscious against a dying horse; knew she had been struck as soldiers battled around her; knew in an instant of clarity what NilokEm was to Telien, what NilokEm had made of her life, saw her enslavement, the beatings, NilokEm's cruel lusting way with her, the baby born and taken from her; saw it all, and in his rage forgot the battle for the runestone and wanted only to kill NilokEm, was across the battlefield grabbing the dark Seer, striking and pounding him, dodging

NilokEm's blows, attacking him with insane fury. The man fell heavy and flailing against him. Ram held him and hit him again and again, then left him unconscious amidst the battle. The stone turned to but a faded rock in NilokEm's hand, a skeleton of the runestone it had been.

Ram shouldered aside soldiers, struck out in fury to reach Telien. Stood looking down at her, shaken at the sight of her. She was so pale, so thin. He lifted her, held her, tried in desperation to revive her. At last he sought a sheltered place between trees where they were somewhat protected from battle, held her and whispered to her until finally she opened her eyes. He could feel her sick confusion, feel the pain of the wound across her forehead, as he examined it. She watched him, pale and uncertain. There was blood clotting, and her forehead was swollen and bruised. He stood holding her, stricken, aware of nothing else, unaware of the shadow moving toward them from deeper in the wood. He was desperate in his fear for her, tried to sense the damage the wound had done, felt her tears on his cheek. He knew her shame at having lain with NilokEm, her pain. He knew her mourning for her lost child. He felt her shame and yet her surging joy in him, her very soul a part of his.

The shadow drew closer. It, too, carried a shard of the runestone; yet it was drawn inexorably by the shard Ram held and the shard NilokEm held, seemed unable to distinguish between the gray, lifeless shard and the live runestone shining deep green in Ram's closed fist. Ram stared at the jade absently, unaware of the shadow, and shoved it in his tunic, held Telien close to him against all harm.

The wraith approached NilokEm first, stood over the fallen Seer sensing out and felt only then the lifelessness of the shard. In anger, it reached down its cold hands, then drew back when NilokEm opened his eyes to stare up at it.

Slowly NilokEm rose, a bull of a man, seething now with hatred, mindless with fear of the powers that had risen uncontrollably around him. He stared at the wraith, drew his knife from his boot, began to stalk the wraith as a creature smaller and weaker than he. And as he drew close to it he knew suddenly and with pounding heart that this deathlike creature carried a shard of the runestone.

He would have that stone.

He dared not think of the destruction of the stone he carried, dared not think of the power that could have done such a thing. Now the stone possessed by this weak creature would be his. The two figures crouched motionless, locked in a gaze of mutual contempt. Of mutual greed. NilokEm's greed was for the runestone, but the wraith's greed was for something else altogether, now that NilokEm's shard of the jade was useless. Its greed was like cold flame, wanting the powerful Seer's body.

Ram watched, frozen; saw the wraith's expression change to sudden pleasure; knew it wanted to die, wanted NilokEm to kill it, that it was aware of nothing now but the closeness of the dark Seer, that it wanted to slip as a shadow into the strong Seer's body. Ram raised his bow. But he was not quick enough, the dark Seer thrust his knife into the wraith's throat; the wraith twisted and fell, its breath gurgling in its severed throat. Ram watched, appalled. He felt the wraith's cold spirit leave that dead body and reach out to enter NilokEm. The dark Seer was aware only then of his danger. He fought with terror, but already he had been weakened. NilokEm struggled against the wraith in desperation, then with growing horror. At last he drew on some deep well of final strength and determination. He lifted his knife and plunged it into his own heart.

NilokEm fell dying, had escaped the wraith in the only way left to him.

The wraith, thwarted and bodiless and in terror for its own existence, turned the darkness of its being suddenly and desperately to enter Ram's body instead, wanted Ram now, this Seer who was master of the stones. Ram battled it, pushed back its questing dark with more strength, even, than he had battled the Pellian Seers when he was a child. Yet he went dizzy under the wraith's growing power, did not understand the increase in that power. Had it drawn strength from the dark Seer as he died? He felt its desperation and drew upon powers he hardly understood in his battle to escape it, to be free of it.

He began to loose its hold at last. He was barely conscious, unaware of the fighting around him or of Telien holding him to her, her knuckles white on his arm where she tried with stubborn will to help him fight. He knew nothing of Skeelie's straining, hard-biting battle to give him power. Yet sick, nearly lost, he rallied finally to drive the wraith out. He felt it go free of him and gasped for air as if he had been drowning. Trying to clear his head, he looked down at Telien.

He saw too late. Saw with cold horror.

Telien had dropped her hands to her sides and was staring up at him with a look of wary hatred. The sense of her being was closed and secret. But her lust for the runestone could not be hidden. She watched Ram greedily. Her beauty, her gentle green eyes, every feature he loved had been changed in an instant to a parody of Telien, horrifying in its greed and coldness.

Sick with shock, Ram watched her kneel over the wraith's thin, abandoned body. He thought only then of the runestone it carried, watched appalled as Telien began to pry its dead fingers apart. He reached for her, but Skeelie was quicker: dark hair flying, she was on Telien reaching for the stone. Telien tore at her, scratching and striking Skeelie across the face. Ram grabbed Telien, sick at hurting her, pulled her off of Skeelie and saw her closed white fist, heard Skeelie gasp, "She has it!" Wincing, he forced Telien's arm back, sick at doing this, amazed at her sudden strength. The pain in her arm seemed to be his own as he pried apart her fingers, took the stone from her; then she was gone from his grasp. Gone once more into Time. He stared at empty space, uncomprehending. A riderless horse lurched past him. The battle erupted nearly on top of him. Ram turned away from it unseeing, his fists clenched around the stone, sick inside himself, tears stinging his eyes.

Somewhere in Time the wraith moved, couched in the fair beauty of Telien. How much of Telien remained, aware and terrified, but unable to escape?

Ram turned back at last and saw Skeelie turn away quickly as if she had been watching him. She was kneeling beside the wraith's body, occupied with pulling the boots off its feet. He stared at her, forgetting his grief for a moment. "You're not going to wear *those!*"

She looked up at him as if she had forgotten he was there, though he knew well enough she had been staring at him caught blindly in his grief. Her face was smeared with dirt and blood. The knot of her dark hair was crooked and loose, hanging against her shoulder. "I have no boots. They're only boots, Ram. My feet are cut and bleeding." Her dark eyes held him; and suddenly they were children again; Skeelie a skinny little girl stealing iron spikes from the smith. It occured to neither of them that their remarks about the wraith's boots were nearly the first words they had spoken to one another in the generations since both of them had been swept away from their own time.

"I will need boots, Ram, if we are to follow her."

Ram wanted to hug her. He remembered her sword then and held it out to her mutely, the silver hilt glinting. Her dark eyes went wide with amazement. Behind them the battle had swept past, not a battle so much now as a mopping up of unhorsed soldiers trying to flee on foot, stumbling over their dead brothers and pursued by wolves and by Hermeth's riders. Ram said, "I took it off a dead Herebian at the foot of Tala-charen."

She ran her finger down the flat of the blade, then sheathed the sword in a quiet ritual, discarding the heavy Herebian one she had used. When she looked up at him, her eyes were deep. "I missed it, Ram. I missed it quite a lot."

THE BATTLE WAS ENDED. Hermeth's soldiers stripped the bodies of valuables and dragged them to a common grave scraped out of the loose loam of the woods. Skeelie's image-wolves were gone. Only the real wolves remained, licking their wounds from battle. Five wolves were dead, lost to the battling armies. *They will live again,* Fawdref said, ignoring Ram's grief for them. *They will live again, Ramad, in the progression of souls. Perhaps as men—or perhaps they will be luckier,* he said dryly, nudging Ram. Ram cuffed him on the shoulder.

"Those dead ones fought for Hermeth, for the stone, Fawdref. Your wolves fought bravely."

*We fought for all of us, Ramad, just as we fought at the Castle of Hape. Just as we fought for Macmen. Never forget, Ramad; it is our battle too. Men are not the only sufferers when the dark grows strong upon Ere.*

Ram knelt suddenly and pressed his face against Fawdref's rough shoulder, reassured by Fawdref's warm, solid presence.

The old wolf was silent for a few moments. Then he looked away across the wood. *Those who have been buried in the common grave, who came from the time of NilokEm, are gone now, Ramad. Only traces of dry, rotting bones remain in the earth where, a moment ago, they lay still warm from recent life. And look behind you at NilokEm's skeleton. His hand still holds the lifeless gray stone that is also a skeleton, lifeless body of the runestone. That stone will vanish too, as, in his own time, the live jade is lifted from his bloody palm to be passed on to his heir who was NilokDal, and to come at long last down to Hermeth's hand—that jade that lies now in your tunic, Ramad.*

# Part Three

*The Lake of Caves*

*Dark mysteries surround the history of Hermeth and surround his victory in the wood of the dark tower south of Dal. Time-flung raiders died in that wood and turned to bone ages old, crumbling before Hermeth's eyes. And a Seer of light came out of a spell-casting to fight by Hermeth's side. Some said the Seer was Ramad of wolves, as the song of that battle tells. Most folk say that could not be. But surely that Seer led wolves: two score great wolves fought by his side to defeat the street-bred rabble and to defeat mysterious warriors. Some say that Hermeth defeated on that battlefield his long-dead ancestor, NilokEm.*

*Surely Hermeth returned victorious to Zandour with a dark-eyed Seer riding beside him and surrounded by running wolves. And there was celebration in Zandour for the victory of free men. But then in Zandour came tragedy to Hermeth. A tragedy no Seer could undo.*

From *The Fourth Book of Zandour*
Writer unknown.

# Chapter Eight

IT WAS a rare good night of feasting and singing. The hall of Hermeth's rough stone villa was crowded with tables laden nearly to overflowing with meats and breads and delicacies brought from all around the city by the townsfolk: shellfish from Zandour's coast baked in leaves of tammi; breads of mawzee grain and whitebarley and wild grass seed; and great custards of tervil and vetchpea and dill. A huge fire blazed on the hearth, roasting chicken and chidrack and wild pig from out the marshes and haunches of deer and sheep. Folk heaped their plates high and carried them to the courtyard, where singing and gay music stirred the night, and the dancing was wild and fast, celebrating Zandour's victory.

How long they had awaited this day; how eagerly they had anticipated the time when they could tend their flocks on Zandour's green hills without fear of Herebian raiders, could sleep at night beneath the peaceful silence of Ere's cool moons, not listening every moment for the sounds of raiders descending from dark hills to burn and steal and kill. There would still be danger. Zandour must still maintain guards and patrols, and the army must train as ever. But not danger as it had been. The street-rabble Seers were slaughtered. Neither Hermeth or Ram could sense any lingering taint of them. The only evil that threatened now was the common strain of straggling raiders never caught up in the Pellian warring, small Herebian pilferers that Zandour could easily deal with.

Zandour showed its pleasure in joyful celebration. The songs sung were mostly the old songs, "Smallsinger Tell Me," "Jajun Jajun," "The Goosetree of Madoc," songs from the coastal lands. Then a young bard made a song about the war in the dark wood, sang the words amidst a sudden stillness as Zandour's people went hushed; and long would it be sung in Zandour. It told of the two stones that were one stone, of Ramad of wolves come out of Time to fight by Hermeth's side; of NilokEm, the dark ancestor, and of Telien, who was mother to Hermeth's grandfather, come suddenly into that wood. It did not speak of the wraith, for only a few had seen that shadow and understood what it was. The song did not tell where Telien had gone, once she disappeared from the wood.

Ram did not join the festivities. He took supper alone beside the hearth in the great hall, his back to the crowds that came to load their plates. He ignored Skeelie, who lurked by a window watching him. He wished she would go away, wanted only his own lonely company. He ate quickly, hardly tasting the deer meat and the carefully prepared dishes, then wandered out of the hall and through the crowds, unaware of the music and jostling. It was to the quiet dark beyond the stables and outbuildings that he was driven by his taut, violent agitation.

Skeelie wanted to follow him and knew he would not tolerate that. He was utterly closed to her in a remoteness that not even friendship could bridge; so awash with suffering for Telien, so deeply grieving. She saw him disappear into shadow and stood in the courtyard for a long time alone after he had gone. Like him, she was unaware of the crowds around her, of the gaiety; and at last she found her way to the room Hermeth had given her.

She shut the door, stood with her back to it, letting the tension ease, letting the sense of isolation, the emptiness of the big square room soothe her. A bathing tub had been brought in, which steamed invitingly. She sat for a while in a deep chair beside the fire, admiring the tapestries and the bright Zandourian rugs, thinking of Ram and of Telien, too lazy even to get into the bath, then began at last to strip off her boots and her borrowed dirty leathers.

The steaming tub felt so good; the aches of battle and the tired stiffness were slowly eased away. She took up the thick sponge, then the ball of perrisax soap, sniffing it with delight, and in a pleasant fog began to scrub off the blood and dirt of battle. When finally she dozed, the water in the tub grew cold and the low fire burned to embers.

RAM WANDERED ALONE in the dark between the outbuildings and pens. He could smell the pigs plainly, and the goats. The music and singing faded to an almost-tolerable blur. He could have done without it altogether. Hermeth had taken one look at his black expression and left him. Skeelie had hung around, annoying with her silent concern. He felt a twinge of guilt. Well, but Skeelie understood. She always knew his pain. Yes, and that in itself was annoying. He stared up at the sky, immense and distant, and cold desolation touched him, the reality of Telien's fate sickening him nearly to madness: Telien, captive in a horror worse than any death could be; Telien trapped now as he had never dreamed possible. Was she aware of her possession yet unable to battle it? Or had her spirit been crippled, or destroyed?

HERMETH FOUND Ram some time later still among the sheep pens and sties. He went to stand beside him, stared absently at the waning moons, watched pale clouds blow across the stars. The singing came faint and cool, muffled by stables and grain rooms. Neither spoke. Ram leaned tiredly against the sty fence, and Hermeth watched him. Ramad of wolves. Ramad, hardly aged since he fought by Macmen's side twenty-three years gone. The clouds shifted to cover the moons, then uncovered them suddenly so moonlight marked the flaming hair of the two Seers. Ram's olive skin and dark eyes and the slight dishing of his face were in sharp contrast to Hermeth's paler, square face and clear blue eyes fringed with pale lashes. Hermeth uncapped a flask of honeyrot. Ram sipped at it absently. Hermeth frowned. "You cannot tear yourself from the image of her, Ramad, from the horror of her possessed. You will not rest until you have followed her. But you . . ." Hermeth took a sip of the honey-rot and capped it. "You do not know how or where to look, how to find your way into Time in the direction she—the wraith—has taken."

Ram nodded, caught in misery. He stared bleakly into the night.

"There is a story in Zandour about a man called the Cutter of Stones. It is said by some that he is evil. I do not believe that. I think he is a magical person."

Ram turned for the first time to look directly at Hermeth.

"A Seer, yes," Hermeth answered his silent question. "But a Seer with special skills. It is said that he cut, from one large stone, five golden stones called starfires that could . . ." He was stopped by Ram's look. "What did I say? Why does the mention of starfires—?"

"Don't stop! Get on with your story!"

"It—it is a tale from herders in Moramia. Five starfires that can hurl a man into Time and carry him—well, just carry him. . . ." Hermeth swallowed. "But you have already been carried into Time." He watched Ram with slow realization. "You—you carry the starfires! You . . ."

Ram reached into a fold of his tunic, drew forth his hand, and held it palm up so the faint light of the moons caught gleaming upon three pale amber stones, cut and faceted, their cool light increasing, deepening at their centers then blazing out suddenly like fire. "Starfire," Hermeth breathed, staring. "Then, Ramad, you have known the Cutter of Stones."

"No. The starfires were given me by another. A man called Anchorstar. He said they were given to him by someone he trusted, but he did not name that man. Perhaps it was the Cutter of Stones, perhaps not. Tell me of the Cutter of Stones."

"It is said the Cutter of Stones can shape Time to his own uses when he chooses."

"Where can I find such a man?"

"It is told that one cannot find him, cannot seek him out,

that he dwells outside of Time and will bide you come to him only if he chooses. But with those starfires—if they can touch Time, can't you . . ."

"The starfires seem sometimes to lead me, but more often only to confuse and twist that which I attempt. Though—though perhaps, after all, they led me to you. Perhaps it was the starfires that led us into the dark wood where Telien—where Telien . . ." Ram bent his head. "I do not know." He stared at the starfires coldly, then said with pent-up anger, "Led me to Telien too late." He looked up at Hermeth. "Could—could this Cutter of Stones be evil?" He dropped the starfires into his tunic with sudden distaste. "Tell me all you know of him."

"I know little more. It is said that if you need him, and if he deems your need a true one, he will call you out of Time to come to him." Clouds raced across the moons in white veils, and as Hermeth turned to look up, a sudden vision came around them, cold as winter. The sty fence disappeared, the villa. The land itself seemed to swim and fold around them and shadows raced across it sparked with silver light. Other, denser shadows rose as a fog might rise from hidden ground, shadows that were figures surging together in the midst of ephemeral winds; they saw young Seers, Children of Ynell, many and many of them: Children soon to be born, perhaps already conceived, Children walking out across Ere carrying light within their souls. Hermeth and Ram saw them struck down, saw them flee before dark warriors; flee to Carriol or northward up over the wild black peaks away from Ere into the unknown lands. They saw other Children living in silence, hiding their skills for fear of death.

They saw Children lying as if dead, asleep with some mind-bending drug, lying on stone slabs in a dark underground place. And the very breath of the wraith pervaded that place so that Ram almost cried out. Did Anchorstar, too, lie there bound in mindlessness? Surely the sense of him was there; but then the vision faded.

119

For long afterward, Ram could not free his mind from the inexplicable weight of that vision.

SKEELIE DOZED and woke in a cold tub. She got out shivering, wrapped herself in a blanket, and huddled before the dead fire. When at last she stirred up the embers and laid on new kindling she felt muzzy, vaguely hungry, and wished she had eaten more supper. Streaks of light came through the shuttered windows and snatches of song from the courtyard, muted and pleasant. She huddled to the fire and soon began to feel warmer, crouched there absently admiring the bright colors of the Zandourian rugs, the pattern of the bedcover. The bed linen, turned back white and smooth, invited her. She rose at last, yawning, and began to prowl the room. In a corner behind a dressing screen, new leathers had been laid out for her, and fresh underlinen, a soft wool tunic, new boots. The sight of them, and the thought of Hermeth's kindness, made tears come suddenly and surprisingly. Someone cared. She caught her breath in a sob that amazed her and stood clutching the leathers, bawling like a child.

Why should someone's kindness make her cry? You're tired, Skeelie! Stop it! Stop crying and get into bed! Yet she knew she was not crying just over the clothes and Hermeth's kindness, that she was crying for Ram, for a kind of gentleness that Ram could never show her.

If only Ram needed her now—as a friend. Instead of going off alone. At last, exhausted with crying, she climbed into bed. In spite of her misery, she took pleasure in the clean sheets, appreciated the gentle softness of the bed. Wriggling down, she let the bed soothe and ease her, clutched the pillow to her and slept almost at once.

For nine days they remained in Zandour, idle as sheep, eating prodigious and succulent meals, riding the countryside just for the pleasure of it, sleeping long and unbroken nights. Skeelie took so many hot baths her skin seemed permanently wrinkled; she luxuriated in her comfortable room, in her new leathers, and in the simple new gowns Hermeth brought to her. Her body began to feel like something human again, fed and clean and rested, the scabs and little wounds healing, and pampered with soft fabrics. Her senses were pampered with the handsome, well-furnished hall—not elegant but well appointed—with the bright tapestries and rugs, and with the neat farms of Zandour and the rolling green sheep pastures. How long such an idyll might last was impossible to guess. Skeelie simply soaked it all up while she could. Though Ram did not do the same. In spite of good meals and the luxuries he had long been without, he was morose, steeped in painful thoughts of Telien. Even occupied with teaching Hermeth the ways of the runestone, Ram had too much time to think; he would sit in the evenings alone beside the fire, preferring his own company and silence, or go skulking off into the night by himself in spite of anything Skeelie and Hermeth might think of to divert him.

The wolves were seldom seen; they had gone to hunt the cliffs up on Scar Mountain, making Skeelie stare away toward that towering mass with a wild, persistent curiosity. The very existence of Scar Mountain there so close, of Gredillon's house only a short ride away, made her taut with questions. What would the house be like if she went there now? In what time had she stood there? Before this time of Hermeth? Or in a time still to happen? She didn't know. It didn't matter; what mattered was that Gredillon's house, or perhaps some power from Gredillon herself, had given her the gift of truly touching Ram's early life. That would always be with her. Had Gredillon sent her the clay bell through some powerful manipulation of Time? And what was Gredillon? White-haired Gredillon—was she one of Cadach's children just as Anchorstar must surely be? Skeelie wondered, if she returned to Scar Mountain now, whether she would find answers to such questions. But she did not return. Something she did not question prevented her, turned her away from that thought, willed her to let the sleeping house be.

Nor did Ram go to Scar Mountain, though surely he must long for the house of his childhood. She could not sense what he felt; his thoughts were closed to her, sunk in desolation. And then on the night of the ninth day, when Ram had been gone longer than usual and it was going on to midnight, Hermeth went to search for him, and did not return.

Skeelie sat immobile beside the fire after Hermeth left her, muzzy with too much honeyrot, disgruntled with Ram's difficult ways, in spite of knowing how he suffered for Telien. She dozed, awakened, dozed again, and still neither Hermeth nor Ram returned. At last she lit a lamp, took up her sword, and went out into the night, her unease making her cross.

She found Ram in the darkness of sheds and sheep pens. Moonlight cast a thin outline across his shoulders where he knelt. What was he doing kneeling beside a sheep pen in the middle of the night? Then she felt, suddenly, the sense of something very wrong, a sense of hollowness; felt Ram's shock and his terrible remorse. Felt the sense of death. Saw then that he knelt beside a body. She went to him without speaking.

Hermeth lay beside the sheep pen, twisted and unnatural in death. Her hands began to shake. She felt the sense of his death like a blow, sudden and sharp, not wanting to believe. Someone she had just been talking with, sitting before the fire with, could not be so suddenly lying dead in the night, in the mud.

But of course he could be. Why had she sensed nothing, back in the hall? She stared at Ram's white, twisted face not understanding anything. When Ram spoke at last, his voice was hoarse and flat.

"She has come here. Telien has come. The wraith—it— has taken the strength from Hermeth. Taken the life from Hermeth." She thought he would drown in his pain. "How can it have become so strong, to do such a thing, Skeelie? I don't understand. It could not have done this before, at Tala-charen." He paused, stared at her. "Did it draw strength from the stones, there in the wood?" His voice was hoarse, near to tears. "Or from NilokEm, before he died? Not—not from Telien. She was so weak, so very frail and weak."

"She was frail of body, Ram. But Telien's spirit—she . . ." Skeelie could not finish.

"When she came out of the night I wanted . . ." He bit his lip, turned his face away. "I wanted only to hold her, to comfort her. I couldn't believe. . . . She was so pale. Great circles under her eyes. She—she was so close to the end of her strength. As if the wraith did not dare let her faint. She—it stood looking at me. It has new power, Skeelie. It has learned to sap the strength from a man like a . . ." Ram swallowed. "Like a lizard sucking out the strength from a creature and leaving a bare shell."

"But she . . ." Skeelie stared at him, knowing suddenly and clearly that the wraith had not come here for Hermeth. "She came for you, Ram."

"She—was so near to failing of strength altogether. The wraith knew he could not get me to kill Telien. Worked it out that it could take a man's strength to replenish itself. Thought that, because Telien and I—because we . . . that it could make me give into it, that it would be easy to drain my body of strength, make me—give myself to her."

She felt a guilty elation that Ram lived, that it was Hermeth lying dead and not Ram. "But how . . . ?"

"Hermeth came upon it—upon us. He battled by my side. We—we battled together, and then suddenly Telien's color heightened, she stood straight, seemed altogether different, healthy, alive. I—I thought she had come back. I thought she had defeated the wraith. I reached out to her. And too late I saw . . ." He drew in his breath. "Too late I saw Hermeth fall. Just—just fall, Skeelie. And she—she reached to put her arms around me, to—to draw me to her. I—I went to her. Wanting her, Skeelie. I knew what she was. She held me. It was . . . I could not let her go. But then I—I began to resist her, to battle her until she drew back. She looked at me with a hatred I can never forget. And then she—she was just suddenly gone." His face filled with pain. "I don't know how long I've been here—how long ago that was. Forever. For Hermeth, it will be forever."

The moons had gone. Ram and Skeelie carried Hermeth's body back to the hall and began to wake Hermeth's men, wake the families who helped in the hall and kitchen. Lamps were lit. Hermeth was laid on a bench in the hall before the dead fire. Those who came knelt immediately, as if no man wanted to stand taller than Hermeth in this moment. Messengers were sent throughout the town.

They made his grave upon a hill at first light. Processions streamed out of the village from all directions in absolute silence: Folk cleanly dressed and carrying little bowls of grain in the traditional gift for the winged horses who might come over Hermeth's grave to speak with him and carrying little bowls of fruit and meats to leave there on his grave for the gods, for if fate smiled, the Luff'Eresi might come too in a last rite to Hermeth. The ceremony itself was simple enough. Ram spoke solemn words, as did Hermeth's lieutenants, the five Seers among them bowing their heads in a last gift of power to Hermeth. Ram held the runestones tight, wanting power for Hermeth now in these moments, wanting to lend Hermeth strength; thought he knew that already Hermeth had left his body, left this place to move into another place and time, another sphere; that there was no need for the power of Seers, of the stones; but still they gave it.

Ram turned away at last from the bare earth that covered the grave like a scar against the green hill. Hermeth's men and the entire city of Zandour followed him down the hill in silence. The wolves, who had come at Hermeth's death down out of Scar Mountain, stood last upon the hill and raised their voices in a wailing lament, in a death song that trembled the sky and would long, long be remembered in

Zandour. And then the wolves came down, too, from Hermeth's grave, and his body was alone there beneath the rising sun.

They would carve and lay a slab of granite, the people of Zandour, to mark the place where Hermeth lay. A little child, staring back up the hill, said, "He can look out now over the sheep meadows." But no one thought Hermeth was there to look out. He was in another place that they could not yet fathom.

"He left no children," Skeelie said, mourning. "No wife—no young Seers."

"There are other Seers, that handful among his lieutenants."

"Untrained. Unskilled, Ram. Just—just those with some power, but not master Seers."

Ram looked down at her, unsettled. "Was I meant to stay here, Skeelie? To use the stones, in his place, to protect Zandour? Or if I can follow Telien, was I meant to leave Hermeth's shard of the runestone behind, to keep only that one taken from the wraith?"

"I don't think you are *meant* to do anything, Ram. Do you think it is all planned out? What do you know you must do?"

He looked at her a long time, a deep look, searching his own soul through what he saw reflected in her eyes. "I will hold these shards of the runestone and keep them, Skeelie. Against the day when the stone will again be whole. And I—I will follow Telien."

That night in the hall, Ram brought together a council of the five young Seers who had ridden as scouts for Hermeth, seeking to understand what skills they had, and to train them.

This five, then, must rule Zandour, for in them lay the needed power. A council of the entire city sat with them, planning; men taking over, as smoothly as they could, the work that had been Hermeth's. Late in the night Skeelie dozed in a chair beside the hall fire, waking only now and then to the men's raised voices. Then suddenly she woke to Ram's hand on her arm, saw that the night had waned and dawn had begun to touch the shuttered windows with gray. Ram stood staring down at her, tired, drawn tight with too much talking. "Get your pack, Skeelie. Put on your boots, your leathers. Take off those silly sandals. I want . . ." He turned to stare northward as if he could look through the very walls of the hall. "I want to climb Scar Mountain. I want . . ." The sense of unrest about him, of need, was powerful.

She rose, forcing herself awake, hurried through the hall, and returned shortly dressed in leathers, with her pack and weapons, to find him in the courtyard pacing and restless as a river cat, his own pack and bow slung over his shoulder, eager to be moving. What was drawing Ram so? Simply restlessness? The sudden need to return to his childhood place? A hope of finding Gredillon for some reason? He was strung taut as a bowstring. Surely something spoke to him, something was pulling at him, but she could make no sense of it. She was only grateful that he wanted her to go, too. They started off at once into the faint touch of dawn, north up the first hill of the sheep pastures, Ram striding out impatiently and Skeelie hurrying to keep up. As they climbed, wolves began to come to them out of the darkness, one here, and then two, all in silence, until soon a dozen wolves paced beside them, Fawdref pressing close to Ram, Torc and Rhymannie nuzzling sometimes at Skeelie's arm.

As they climbed, the sense of promise, of beckoning grew strong indeed. On the crest of the hill Ram stopped and turned to watch the dawn sky lighten. Down in the town they could see the dark shapes of wagons and of horses and riders moving in over the hills and roads, as folk from the farther reaches of Zandour began to arrive in Zandour's city to pay their last respects to Hermeth. Ram stood staring down, then silently he drew from his tunic the little pouch he had made of soft white goathide and spilled the two runestones and the starfires out into his palm. He seemed puzzled. Skeelie watched, still and expectant, not knowing what was to happen, but filled with growing excitement. Something was building around them, something of power. She began to feel Ram's curiosity, his questions rising, felt him begin to reach out hesitantly. They stood looking down upon the slowly lighting land, and then, alarmed suddenly, she turned to look back up the mountain, saw the wolves turn too; Ram turned as if someone had spoken his name. He took her shoulder in a sharp grip.

Above them the mountain had become unclear, as fast winds moved down across it sweeping toward them, blurring their vision. Fingers of wind snatched at them, blurring the dawn sky. Then the great body of wind itself was sweeping and pummeling them, ripping at their tunics, laying the wolves' coats and ears flat. Fawdref crouched and snarled; the wind pounded, tore the very grass from the hill, and a rider came racing out of it leading two wild, rearing horses, shouting, "Mount! Mount you, Ramad!" The hooded rider, his cowl bound tight against the bite of the wind, his tall, thin figure leaning from the saddle, urged Ram; and Ram did not pause or question, but grabbed the reins and was in the saddle. Skeelie's fear for him rose like a tide. "No, Ram! Wait!" She leaped for his reins, tried to stop his plunging horse. "Don't follow! You don't know..." Terror of his being swept away, terror of the cowled rider made her scream into the wind as Ram kicked the horse, jerked the reins from her hand and sent his mount into the turmoil alongside the dark rider.

"Oh, don't, Ram. You don't know..." All hint of dawn had disappeared; the wind was dark as midnight. The wolves stood frozen, then suddenly leaped to follow Ram. "Ram..." Skeelie's voice was empty, a whisper blown back in her face. "You don't know where he leads you...." But Ram had disappeared in the storm of wind.

She jerked the reins of the riderless horse until it stood still, then leaped to the saddle and was swept into the dark wind herself. The flanks of the dark mounts were ahead;

then the wolves were running beside her leaping through wind. She stared ahead at the hooded rider. Who *was* this man, racing out of Time's winds to snatch them up like this? She felt his attention, though he had not changed his crouching position over the wethers of his stallion. Then suddenly he straightened in the saddle, brushed back his hood as if annoyed, and turned to look at her, wind whipping his white hair across his face.

Anchorstar?

Was it Anchorstar? Yes, she recognized him now, that long, thin face. He nodded to her and she stared back through the wild wind, cross and suspicious. But she settled down to ride, watching Anchorstar warily, watching Ram's back ahead of her. The tearing speed of the horses increased as the wind increased, and the wolves sped with them across winds that threatened to fling the riders from their saddles into timeless space, washing Skeelie with cold fear, and exciting her to madness. Never was there land, but faces looked out of darkness, and the moons were full, then gone, then new again.

Then the wind died. The night became dense and still. The moons hung like two half coins, casting silver light across the quiet horses where they stood on an open hill beside a wood. The white-haired rider dismounted as casually as if he had just trotted across a farm meadow. He unsaddled his stallion, then turned it loose to graze, ignoring Skeelie and Ram. Picking up sticks from the edge of the wood, he began to lay a fire on the bare slope.

The wolves turned, grinned, then leaped away into the wood. Torc flung back, *To hunt! To hunt for meat, sister!* Skeelie could feel the passionate curiosity among the wolves at being in a new place, could taste for a moment the new smells as Torc did; and she held for a brief moment Torc's wild excitement at the newness, the land virgin to be traveled and tasted and known intimately. Then she dismounted, only slowly recovering from the drunkenness of that wild ride.

Ahead rose immense mountains, washed in moonlight. To her right, the wood was a velvet patch of dark. And to her left, the land dropped down steeply to what seemed, in the moonlight, a very deep chasm or valley. The space around her seemed greater than she had ever known. She felt exposed, threatened by such space; and felt again a cold twinge of unease because Ram had followed so easily. But she was being foolish; Ram knew Anchorstar. She turned to unsaddling her mount. What else did she think Ram would do but follow whatever way might lead to Telien? She reached out to Ram in her mind, but he was oblivious of her in his sudden hope that this wild ride had set him on a course that would bring him soon to Telien.

"Unsaddle your horse, Ramad," Anchorstar said. "He cannot graze with the bit in his mouth. He will come to me when I call. They are Carriol-bred horses, bred from your own stock, Ramad, in years past." He tipped his chin toward the tall dun stallion he had ridden. "Do you not remember him? You tried to buy him once."

Ram pulled himself back from his tumbled thoughts. "I remember him. A horse I would have sold my soul to have."

Anchorstar bent to put flint to the fire. When the blaze had flared, then settled and begun to burn steadily, he produced from his saddlebags a tin kettle, tammi tea, hard mawzee biscuits, mountain meat.

Skeelie hunkered down by the fire, hardly tasting the food she ate, so caught was she in Ram's rising hope, his need to push on, to reach out to Telien; and then in his beginning uncertainty that perhaps Anchorstar would try but *could* not lead him to Telien; and then his growing depression, his returning desolation at the horror of Telien's possession.

"We will sleep here until dawn," Anchorstar said, ignoring Ram's depression, "and then we will push on. We are in a time out of Time, Ramad. We are now in the time of the Cutter of Stones."

Ram stared at him. "How can you move with purpose through Time when I cannot? I could not follow Telien. I have only been buffeted through Time with never any reason until—until it was too late. I could not touch her soon enough, reach far enough back into Time to save her from NilokEm. There is no reason to how I have moved."

"There was reason, Ramad, when you fought to help Macmen, then to help Hermeth." Anchorstar stared into the fire, and Ram did not speak again. Anchorstar said at last, "I do not move us through Time, nor do I pretend to know the intricate patterns that touch such movement. Though I know that I lead you, now, to the Cutter of Stones, lead you by his will. And that through him you can seek the wraith, seek Telien."

"Why do you help me? Why do you care if I find Telien, or if I can save her and destroy the wraith?"

"I am linked to the wraith, even as are you. I do not know why. Perhaps it has to do with my own time. I feel that this is so. I feel certain I must return to my own time, and soon. Something there calls to me, and perhaps the wraith has to do with that in some way I do not yet comprehend."

THE WIND CHANGED in the night to blow icy, down from the mountains. Skeelie woke once to see Anchorstar building up the fire, then slept again. Dawn came too soon, and she woke huddled in her blanket, to watch Ram saddle the horses while Anchorstar came from out the shadowed wood carrying the tin kettle. He gave her a rare smile. "There is a spring there in the wood if you care to wash."

She sat up, pulling the blanket around her. The sky was hardly light. The wood lay in blackness. Ahead, the dark smear of sharp peaks rose against a gray horizon, peaks with a shock of snow at the top. To her left, the hill dropped steeply to the valley far below. She could sense, but not yet see, that a river ran there at the bottom like a thin silver thread. Wild land, and huge, rising up to peaks that must surely be a part of the Ring of Fire.

She rose and went barefoot into the shadowed wood where dawn had not yet come, found the stream twisting cold between the roots of ancient trees, washed herself, shivering, kneeling in shallow rapids. When she came out, dawn was beginning to filter into the wood, and the wolves were there among the trees. She pulled the blanket around her, embarrassed at her nakedness, and rubbed herself dry. Only when the wolves had gone, Fawdref dragging the carcass of a deer over his shoulder, did she remove the blanket to pull on her shift. She could sense Ram finishing with the horses, could feel his mood like a dark pall, knew he had waked with the sense of Telien's captive spirit gripping him. When she returned to the camp, he was surly and rude.

Anchorstar had cooked thin slices of the deer meat on a stick. Ram ate hunched over, not speaking, gulping his food. The morning was bright, the air cold and clear. Skeelie reached out to the aliveness, the wholeness of the rising morning, needing this, needing to put away from her the sense of death and depression Ram carried. Deliberately, she savored the tender deer meat, the tea and warmed bread. But though she tried, she could not rid herself of Ram's misery. She supposed he knew she shared it. Perhaps that made him surlier still. He tossed down his eating tin finally and rose, glowering at her before he went to untie the horses.

She gazed up at the far peaks, crowned with white, feeling miserable herself suddenly, angry at Ram for making her so, and angrier at herself for letting him. Anchorstar laid a hand on her knee in friendship and understanding. She stared into his strange golden eyes, felt his sympathy. His voice was soft. He glanced once to where Ram had already mounted, then looked ahead to the mountains. "This is strange, wrinkled land. There lies ahead a mountain still hidden, we will come on it as we top the next hills. That is our destination, Esh-nen, a mountain capped with ice but with fires deep in its belly, with a lake like a steaming bath. Well, but you will see."

When they set out, Ram's thoughts still ran through Skeelie's mind and would not be stilled. If the wraith was growing stronger so rapidly that it could now suck out a man's life, could they hope to defeat it before it would destroy them? It carried Hermeth's spirit within it now, which made it infinitely stronger; Skeelie remembered its hoarse whisper, there in Gredillon's house, *You will come into me our way, as the others have come. . . .* Could they, even through the Cutter of Stones, follow and destroy that creature of death? The sense of the wraith closed in around her as they started over a rise of boulders, the horses humping in a lurching gallop against the steepness; and then suddenly, coupled with her worry over the wraith and somehow a part of it, she began to feel Anchorstar's restlessness, his growing need to return to his own time. She thought that he could sense something amiss there but not discern its shape; she felt a darkness touching him too painful to bring to view.

At midday the riders came over the last of a series of rises and were facing quite suddenly a great white mountain that sprawled just above the hills like an immense reclining animal. "That is Esh-nen," Anchorstar said. "The white shoulder." The west wind blew the mountain's cold breath down to them. "There in Esh-nen the Cutter of Stones dwells in a place out of Time, a place impervious to Time."

They built a fire for their noon meal and set the meat to cook. Ram stripped the horses to let them graze, then hunched down beside the fire and drew the leather pouch from his tunic. He fished out the three starfires and held them in his palm. They caught the firelight, flashing. He looked up at Anchorstar with taut impatience. "Tell me about the Cutter of Stones. Tell me where he came by the stone from which he cut these, and what he intended for them."

"The Cutter of Stones himself will tell you what he wishes you to know of the starfires, Ramad." Anchorstar shrugged, dismissing the subject. Then he looked at Ram and seemed to soften, adding, "There were five. I carry one still. And Telien carries the other."

"And that one has not helped Telien. Perhaps they are cursed stones."

"I do not think that," Anchorstar said, then grew silent. When at last he spoke again, his words were harder, clipped, as if he in turn had lost patience. "Where is the runestone, Ramad, that Telien brought out of Tala-charen?"

"I do not know. When I held her close to me there in the wood, I caught a sense of it, quick and fleeting. A sense of it in darkness. Lost. As if Telien herself did not remember where."

"And if you were made to choose between the search for Telien and the search for the shards of the runestone—which you vowed once, Ramad, that you would join together again—which path would you choose?"

Ram stared at him for so long it seemed he did not mean to answer. At last he rose, still silent, and walked away from them. When he turned back, his scowl was more lonely than angry; and still for a long moment he did not speak. Then he said only, "You know as well as I, what I would do. What I must do. But it does not help to contemplate that pain before—unless—I must."

He stood silent, seemed to have forgotten them. Then at last, "When I held her, there was a sense of mountains, dark peaks rising: I could feel her despair. I saw the stone in darkness for an instant." He paused, seemed drawn away suddenly, then he looked across at Anchorstar with surprise. "Words come into my mind. Words—unbidden." He began to repeat slowly, then with more assurance, in a kind of prophesy that none of them ever afterward could put a name to except, simply, a moment of Seer's prophesy. "It lies in darkness somewhere, in the north of Cloffi, or in the mountains there." And then his words became trancelike. "Found by the light of one candle, carried in a searching, and lost in terror. Found again in wonder, given twice, and accompanying a quest and a conquering." The cold wind touched them, the fire guttered then sprang bright. Never, even in all the violent visions of his childhood, had words of prophesy sprung clearly into Ram's mind, ringing in his head almost as if spoken by another. Visions had come, scenes, direct knowledge. But not words thundering to be spoken.

He repeated softly the prediction, then turned to Skeelie, suddenly needing her. "Did—could Telien have spoken this into my mind? Could she remember—somehow know . . .?" But then his eyes went dark, his expression turned grim once more. "Telien could not speak such a prediction. She is not a Seer. Such a prediction comes—within a pattern I cannot even imagine. Can any Seer know the pattern by which he takes power?"

Anchorstar emptied the kettle, began to pack up the remains of the meal, then stopped to look at Ram. "A Seer can know the pattern as well, Ramad, as he knows the pattern of the heavings of the earth and the birth and rebirth of souls. We are a part of something, Ramad. The runestones are a part of it. But what that pattern is, or what made it, we do not know. Why can we three move through Time when all men, even all Seers, cannot?" The white-haired Seer fell silent, caught in some private sadness.

Skeelie said softly, very softly, the words of the ancient tree man, ". . . born outside the progression of souls—Those so born can deal with Time sufficiently." The words of the man who was surely Anchorstar's sire. Anchorstar looked at her a long time, a deep, puzzled look. And though she could not read the thoughts that touched him, his face held infinite sadness. As if, though he did not recognize the words, they touched a remote place within his soul, a place of everlasting pain.

# Chapter Nine

FOUR DAYS BROUGHT them up into Esh-nen. It was so cold now, they rode with their blankets around their shoulders and slept close together at night, with the wolves crowded around in a warm cluster. Sleeping close, as she and Ram had sometimes done as children out of fear or in the icy nights on Tala-charen, Skeelie could feel the sense of their friendship grow steadier. She would lie wakeful with the pleasure this gave her, and with annoyance at her own dependence on Ram; but with, sometimes, a longing for him that even this closeness could not quiet. Then she would turn away from Ram and huddle into Torc's shoulder, choking back tears; and Torc would turn and lick her face and lay her muzzle into Skeelie's neck. *You suffer too violently, sister. Time will take away the pain.*

*It never can.*

Torc could not answer her, for her own pain, the memory of her dead cubs and the pain of her lost mate, had not abated. Together they would lie miserable and wakeful in the cold, still night, sharing their loneliness. Ram slept beside her unknowing, and Anchorstar, if he knew, did not speak of it. The very beauty of the night in this barren place, the moonlight like crystal on the jutting rocks, seemed to make her misery even sharper.

The world seemed to have grown larger and more remote as they ascended. And while at first this had increased Skeelie's loneliness, soon the immense spaces began to fascinate her, as if they held within themselves powerful and hidden meanings. She began to touch within herself new plateaus of strength that came sharper still as the peaks rose higher and wilder around them.

The ground over which they rode seemed never to have known spring, seemed always to have been as now, frozen

135

and barren of life. The snow, which had at first lay in patches on the frozen ground, increased to a heavy blanket. They dug moss from beneath the rock cliffs for the horses, and Anchorstar took from his pack precious rations of grain for them, but still the animals began to grow gaunt. It was a bleak, heartless mountain. The few trees stunted along the edges of the rising cliffs might have clung there forever, unchanged. The sense of their own smallness became nearly unbearable. The mountain stretched around them white and cold and silent.

Anchorstar, too, became silent, as remote as the spaces surrounding them, so Skeelie felt that at any moment he might fade altogether to become a part of the empty vastness through which they traveled.

Soon the snow was so deep the horses had to fight their way. Then the riders dismounted to trample down a path and make the way easier for the mounts. They kept on so, walking, their feet growing cold, their boots sodden, stopping again and again to dig packed snow from the horses's hooves. The wolves alone found it easy to move swiftly across the whiteness. They brought meat—rock hare and a small deer—so there was no need for the travelers to hunt.

They came, at evening of the sixth day, up over a rising snow plain to a ridge. Beyond it, the land dropped suddenly, falling down to a deep blue lake far below. A lake not frozen over, but breathing hot steam against ice-covered cliffs. They began to descend, the horses slogging through deep snow sideways, held back from overbalancing by a short lead. Soon they could feel the lake's warm breath. The rising steam grew thick around them, turning to fog in the cold air, hiding the snow-clad mountains. They descended into a cauldron of fog, of shifting pale shadows and then of unexplained darknesses rising and stretching away like voids between the clouds of mist.

Skeelie could feel Anchorstar's tenseness. He seemed reluctant suddenly, and at the same time almost eager. She heard him whisper words indistinguishable, then speak a name. "Thorn!" Then, "That Seer is Thorn of Dunoon!" A wind caught the heavy fog and swirled it into patterns against darkness. Suddenly they were not standing in snow, but on a narrow rocky trail winding along the side of a bare, dark mountain, black lava rock rising jagged against the sky. The horses were gone. The air was warm, a warm breeze blew up from the valley below. Time lay asunder once again, twisted in its own mysterious convolutions, and they had been carried with it like puppets, swept away from their destination. Skeelie responded with anger, this time with a sense of betrayal.

Below them lay pastures green as emeralds, and a little village, its roof thatch catching the last light of the setting sun. Below that village, down at the foot of the mountain, they could see a city. Surely they had come to the mountains above the village of Dunoon. No city that Skeelie knew, save Burgdeeth, lay so close to the foot of the Ring of Fire. A flock of goats was being herded up into the high pastures, the herder a young redheaded Seer; and suddenly Skeelie went dizzy. Time shifted again, darkness was on the mountain. Though they could still see the herder, who stood in moonlight now, his goats grazing among black boulders. Anchorstar sighed.

"We are in my own time, and I know I must move in this time." His words came heavy, as if he were very tired. Then his voice lifted. "That young Seer—can't you feel it? Yes—he is linked with the runestone!" He was tense with excitement, now, stood staring down eagerly. "He is linked with the runestone that Telien carried. The runestone that Telien brought out of Tala-charen."

Ram had caught his breath, stood watching, sensing out.

"He will touch that stone," Anchorstar continued. "I feel certain of it. He is linked with your prophesy, Ramad. *Found by the light of one candle, carried in a searching....* Linked in a way I cannot fathom. But Ram..." Anchorstar laid a restraining hand on Ram's arm.

137

"Telien is not in this time, nor does he know of her—nor do I feel that she will come to this time. That young Seer—I think he is hardly aware of his gift. It is an ignorant time, ignorant!" And then, his voice fading, "Kubal is rising. Can't you feel their dark intent?"

He was gone, mountain and valley gone. Ram and Skeelie stood alone in fog and snow, freezing cold, the blue lake below. Anchorstar's horse was gone, its hoofprints ending suddenly in the deep snow just where Anchorstar's footprints ended. Their own two horses pressed close to them, shivering.

An after-vision filled their minds with Anchorstar, not on that dark mountain now but riding the dun stallion along a flat green marsh next to the sea. "He is in Sangur," Ram breathed. "Surely those are the marshes of Sangur. How...?" He stared at Skeelie. "What mission must he now endure, in order to make his way back to the mountains, and to that young Seer? *Is* there sense of it, Skeelie?"

She could not answer him. They stood staring at one another, caught between wonder and fear at the forces that moved around them, that flung them so casually across Time. Was there sense to it, reason? She remembered, suddenly and vividly, standing with Ram inside the mountain Tala-charen, could hear his voice, a child's voice, yet very certain of the words he spoke. *There is one force. But it is made of hundreds of forces. Forces balance, overbalance— that is what makes life; nothing plans it, that would take the very life from all—all the universe. It is the strength of force in our desires for good and evil, Skeelie, that makes things happen...*"

He touched her thoughts. She whispered, "Do you still believe that?"

"I—I don't know. Sometimes I do. Sometimes I'm not sure how much. I guess—I guess I have more questions now than I did then. Anchorstar is gone. He brought us to this place and is gone. What forces...?" He looked at her long and deep, then at last they turned in silence, the sense of their wondering flashing between them, but no words adequate to answer such questions. They looked down at the lake, wreathed in mist, then started down toward its shore.

As they descended, snow turned to ice, for all was frozen here where the lake's steam melted the snow again and again, then cold winds froze it. The far steep shore glistened with ice, rising up to the mountains. Their boots broke through the thin layer of constantly melting and refreezing crust, and the horses pawed, sidestepping, uncertain and suspicious, moving one wary step at a time. Across the lake, the shore was riddled with caves, visible now and then through the mist, and there seemed to be caves beneath the water, too, dark, indistinct patches.

At the lake's edge Skeelie knelt, scooped warm water into her cold hands, then plunged her face in, came up dripping. The wary horses settled to drink at last as the wolves crowded around them to lap up the clear, warm water. For some moments, no one saw or sensed the man who stood in the shelter of a snowbank watching them, a big man swathed in white furs, nearly invisible against the snowbank. Fawdref sensed him first, sprang around suddenly, snarling, ready to leap. But then he stopped, did not advance on the stranger.

The man pushed aside the flap of white fur that had covered his face and stared down at the wolf with eyes like fierce black embers. Within the white hood, his face was a dark oval, sun-browned, creased with lines, craggy, his black beard clipped in a square manner, sharply defined. His dark eyes smiled suddenly, eyes filled with depths that seemed to engulf them all as completely as the warp of Time could engulf them. Skeelie fought his power, wanted to pull away; yet his strength remained aloof, did not crush her as she felt it could easily do. He said abruptly, without preamble, "Come then," turned from them and started around the icy shore, never doubting that they would follow him.

They went in single file, Ram leading his mount, then Skeelie leading hers, the wolves coming behind, austere and silent. The only sound was the crunch of frozen snow as they made a solemn journey around the lake to where a white hill lay, a long mound with smoke rising from its center. The power of the man drew and enfolded Skeelie until she no longer wanted to be rid of it. She did not attend to how his power affected Ram, so caught was she in the sense of this man who was the Cutter of Stones.

As they drew close to the white mound, they could see a white door in its side. The Cutter of Stones pushed that door open, and they entered through the wall of snow into an inner court, open to the sky. Log outbuildings and stables stood on three sides of the court, their roofs covered with high banks of snow. A long, low house of heavy logs flanked the right side, snow roofed.

Two stalls had been made ready for their horses, with dry grass and grain and leather buckets of fresh water. The goats and sheep in the other stalls watched with marble eyes as Skeelie led her bay gelding into a stall and unsaddled him. She was tired suddenly, aching with weariness. Perhaps a weariness born of the intense isolation of this place— outside of Time, outside of any world they knew. Or perhaps it was a weariness born of her sure knowledge that she and Ram moved now, inevitably, toward crises in their lives, toward turning places. She was not sure she was ready for any kind of crisis. At this moment, all she wanted was a drink of something hot and supper and a warm bed. She began to rub the saddle marks from the gelding's back. He ate greedily. When she turned from him at last, Ram was leaning in the doorway.

She studied him, his brown eyes, his olive skin glowing now from the cold, the long, thin bones of his face, unruly thatch of red hair. Wanting to touch his cheek, she shielded her thoughts from him, feeling stupid and ashamed of her love for him, because he could not return it.

"We are farther than the end of the world, Skeelie. Farther than any world, maybe. Farther..." His jaw clenched, pushing back the pain of Telien.

"You let it eat at you, Ram! What good—you..." She turned from him, furious, then was ashamed all over again. What was she so angry about? He couldn't help it. She was tired, needed a hot meal, a bath. She turned back, took his hand and pulled him out into the courtyard. It was starting to snow. The wolves rose from around the door like a pack of great dogs, grinned and were off through the court and up the side of a hill to hunt. Ram dropped her hand, was unaware he did so, or that he had been holding it. She stared at him reproachfully. There was nothing she could do to make him aware of her when he did not want to be. And nothing she could do to relieve his pain for Telien. She could only stay beside him and help him search and do whatever was needed. *Doormat!* she thought angrily. *Doormat!* But it was what she wanted to do, must do, or life would have no meaning. When he had found Telien, when they had gone off together—if they could save her, if they could release her from the wraith—then, Skeelie thought, she could dissolve into self-pity, and after that make a new life for herself. Now there was only the search for Telien, and it didn't matter if she was a doormat.

They entered the hall. Skeelie dropped her pack by the door, thankful to be rid of the weight. The warmth of the great room and of the blazing fire engulfed them. It was a huge, square room with three log walls, and a fourth of stone where a fire blazed beneath a deep stone mantel. Rafters thick as a man's waist caught the reflection of leaping flames. Cushions were stacked before the hearth, and beside them a low table made of some dark, dull wood. There was no other furniture. Fur hides and fur cushions were strewn in piles about the room. A black stewpot hung to one side of the fire. The Cutter of Stones was stirring this.

He had removed his white furs, was clad now in a plain brown tunic and trousers. His dark eyes saw Skeelie clearly, saw her aching tiredness, her hunger, her discouragement. He held out steaming mugs to them, a heady brew scented with spices. And all the time, he looked directly at Skeelie. His voice was deep, comforting. "I am called Canoldir." Then, "Come Ramad, make yourself comfortable before the fire." Ram turned from them.

Canoldir looked at Skeelie so long she felt a blush rising. At last he took her arm and guided her through the hall to a corridor and down this to a chamber. He did not speak, but his very presence seemed to rest and strengthen her. "This room opens onto the lake. There is no one about, you may bathe. Supper will be ready when you are." He turned away, was gone; she felt only the sense of his mind, for a moment still watching her. Then she was quite alone. She pushed the door closed behind her and stood surveying the room.

It was large and square though not nearly so huge as the hall. There were a few pieces of simple furniture, a big bed covered in a red woven tapestry, other tapestries hanging against the log walls. In one wall was a great window, opening nearly to the floor, made of hundreds of small panes of precious glass. It looked out on the lake and the icy shore.

There was a fur robe lying across a bench, along with fur slippers and linen towels. She stripped down at once, pulled the robe around her and stepped barefoot through the window out into the snow. Her feet began to tingle from the cold, a strangely exhilarating, comforting feeling. She stood for a moment at the edge of the lake, staring up through scarves of steam at the white mountains, watching the first stars come in the deepening sky, her mind on Canoldir. At last she slipped out of the robe and dove in one motion into the water, luxurious in its warmth, rolled languidly, then dove deep, felt the aching tiredness leave her. Finally she struck out in a long line across the lake, sharply aware of the contrast between the warm water and the icy bite of air across her cheek and lifting arms and shoulders.

At the far shore, close to the caves, she dove again and peered into shadowed grottoes. Then, in a little pool beneath snowbanks she floated on her back staring up through steam and past ice-crusted cliffs at the first stars. When she rolled over again, a vision came so suddenly and sharply it shocked her. So clear, so very real! She stood in a hut made all of saplings, stood beside a center fire pit and held a babe in her arms; the love and warmth that filled her was nearly too much to bear. A babe urgently important, not only because of the love she felt, but because of much more; though what, exactly, she could not sense.

The vision vanished. She floated between icy banks, feeling the loss of that child like a wound.

Whose child? Whose child had it been? And when, in what time?

She swam back at last to the white hill. She could see now that the window through which she had come was partly hidden from the lake by a jutting snowbank. When she stepped from the water, the icy air made her tingle. She pulled on her robe and made her way absently through the snow, thinking of the child she had held.

Once inside she returned to the large hall dressed in the long fur robe and fur slippers, deliciously soft against her clean skin. The low table had been set with wooden plates and with a loaf of warm new bread, a pot of ale, a garnish of some pale, long-leafed vegetable that she did not recognize, and the steaming stewpot set on a metal trivet. She settled herself on cushions opposite Canoldir and looked around the room with appreciation.

Canoldir's weapons hung beside the fireplace: a fine sword, knives, a beautiful bow, arrows with game tips. Canoldir watched her careful appraisal. "There is game on these snowy peaks, Skeelie. Stag and small deer and a great cowlike animal that wanders the snowbanks in search of moss. There are sheltered valleys where they can dig deep for fodder, and valleys where the burning heart of the mountain gives forth heat enough for the grass to grow thick. There is game in plenty, and I speak a prayer for them when I must kill them."

She saw then that across the mantel, beneath Canoldir's weapons, were carven five faint lines of words. She rose, stood before the blazing fire to read them.

> *Those who have torn away the seams of Time,*
> *through the repetition of their birth upon Ere,*
> *can move through the tapestry of Time*
> *and can weave new powers into the intricate fabric*
> *of the one power.*

When she turned, Canoldir was dishing up the stew. She watched him, caught up in the words. What was their meaning? So like the tree man's words, *born outside the progression of souls. . . .*

She came to the table abstracted, seated herself on the low cushion with her feet tucked under her robe. The stew smelled wonderful, rich and brown. Canoldir cut bread for her, said quietly, "Why do those words worry you? Do you not understand them?"

"I'm not sure. That—that though most are born again in different lives, different worlds, some are born twice upon Ere? But then . . ." She saw that Ram had read the words, had puzzled over them. She waited for him to speak.

"Those born so have woven a new pattern into the warp of powers. And so we—you, me, Telien, Anchorstar—have woven a new pattern that can reach through Time." Ram looked to Canoldir for agreement.

"Yes."

"But then the wraith . . ." Skeelie began.

"The wraith makes a new pattern yet again. And, one would hope, not a lasting pattern, but one that will fray and fade." Canoldir reached to refill their mugs with hot brew.

"But why were we born a second time upon Ere?" Skeelie said. "And the Luff'Eresi are so born, too. I don't—"

"The Luff'Eresi are a different matter," Canoldir said, watching her again. "And the Luff'Eresi are not, as were you and Ram, born a second time of the same race." He felt her puzzlement. "Nothing *made* the repetition of your birth, Skeelie. Your birth is chance. Only chance. The very repetition is a new thread woven into the warp of an incomprehensible pattern. A pattern born of chance, but fitting and meaningful beyond anything we can imagine."

They ate in silence for some time, Ram and Skeelie puzzling over questions that interlocked even as the forces that touched them interlocked. At last Canoldir began to speak again, to speak of Time and of things both strange and familiar, then soon of things so remote that both Ram and Skeelie were caught with fascination in the rising web of his words. And as he spoke his moods were as changing as quicksilver, and with each mood, his face, his whole presence changed. He might have been a dozen men, some terrifying in their fury when he spoke of the dark Seers or of evils across Ere, some as innocent and filled with joy as a young colt. When there was joy, Canoldir's dark eyes shone with clear light. When he spoke of evil upon Ere, his eyes were a killer's eyes.

He showed them Time in so far distant a past that men had not yet come into Ere, a time when only the triebuck and the great cats, the snow tigers and white-horned beasts and animals with long slim necks and hides like saffron roamed Ere. And great dark beasts, neither bull nor bear, dwelt among the woods and fields of Ere; and then his eyes laughed with pleasure. He showed them a time when the first Cherban peoples came into Ere from across the sea, just as the old myths told, and sank their ships at the point of Sangur's coast in solemn ritual and spoke no more of those ships or of the land from whence they had come. He showed them the Cherban making settlements along Ere's coasts, and then showed the Cherban decimated by death and slavery as the first Herebian raiders came down out of the high desert lands. He showed them the young Cherban herder, Ynell, who was the first in whom the Seer's powers rose, the first to speak with the gods; and then they saw how the Seeing grew among the Cherban peoples from that latent talent, suddenly catching fire among them at Ynell's persecution and at the growing threat from the Herebian raiders. "But that," Canoldir, said, "that was long ago."

Then he showed them, abruptly, a vision of Telien that made Ram catch his breath and draw away from them in painful silence.

"Yes, Ramad, you search for Telien. You search for the wraith of the dead Yanno, who gave his soul to the drug MadogWerg in the caves of Kubal. Who would have destroyed Anchorstar and many more, except for the skill of a few young Seers—young Seers wielding the runestone that Telien brought with her out of Tala-charen."

Ram stared at him. "The runestone she . . . but then that runestone is found!" He watched Canoldir, perplexed. "She had—she did not remember."

"Telien did not—will not find it. And that time is yet to come, Ramad, in the way of your lives. I could tell you that that runestone is found in that future time; and yet all Time can change at the whim of forces that even I—who move outside of Time—cannot understand truly. Let us say that that stone is, in all likelihood, found." He paused, watching them; then idly he began to brush the crumbs from the sliced bread into a little heap and spread them out with one deft movement of his palm, began to draw in the thin veil of crumbs, one thin line across, bisected by another. When he looked up at last, he had scribed the little circle of crumbs into nine sections, eight fanning out, and one in the center. Ram sat staring at the sketch. Skeelie was silent, following Ram's thoughts. Just so had the shattered runestone of Eresu lain in Ram's palm, in nine jagged pieces. "It had a center stone," Ram said with amazement. "I remember now; but I did not remember. I remembered well that there were nine shards of jade, but not that one was a center stone. Gone. Gone from my mind. I see it clearly now, one long, oval stone. The center—the core of the runestone." He raised his eyes to Canoldir. "A golden stone—amber..."

"Yes, Ramad. The core of the runestone, just as Time has a core about which it weaves endlessly."

Ram drew from his tunic the leather pouch and spilled its contents onto the table. The two jade runestones. The three starfires. But suddenly the starfires were four. His hand paused in midair. He looked up at Canoldir again with cold shock. "Telien's starfire? Telien's... *You* brought it here! *Is Telien*..."

"It is Anchorstar's," Canoldir said quietly. "Anchorstar has no need for such a stone now. Anchorstar moves in his own time, thirty years beyond the time in which you mourned and buried Hermeth of Zandour, Ramad. Perhaps Anchorstar may move in Time yet again, but only shallow slips through Time, I feel. I think that he will not need the power of the starfire in that time to which he truly belongs. That time in which he was bred by Cadach. For Cadach, too, born twice upon Ere, wandered Time, bred his children through Time, in different times by different women, before he turned his powers into an evil that was his undoing.

"The starfire belongs with you, Ramad. You have need for all the starfires together, in the semblance of the one stone. Perhaps that need in part is simply to signify that in some time yet to come, you will join the stone itself. Make it whole again."

"You seem very certain."

"I am not certain. But if your powers seek out sufficiently well, if your powers, your commitment, are strong enough, unswerving enough—then that very force can change and realign forces moving upon Ere, can well bring you, at some time not yet clear, into the realm of all the shards of the jade. And then, Ramad, all powers may align with you— the powers you can touch but do not fully comprehend. If you are strong enough, all powers may draw in as they did at the splitting of the jade, atop Tala-charen. But this time the jade might be fused again into one whole stone. I do not say this *will* happen. I say that it is possible. It will depend on you. There is something in your blood, in your breeding, that belongs to the stone and its joining."

"If all depends on me, is Anchorstar's mission of no concern then? Does he search for that one stone in vain?"

"Anchorstar's mission is urgent. All powers, all forces, must move as one, Ramad. You may be the last key in the final joining, or someone close to you may. But the powers and strengths of all who move in this battle are of urgency. Anchorstar's mission is a part of the whole; the mission that consumes him now is to battle that which has gone awry. He moved with such intensity that he has all but forgotten that which has occurred before. Other times have become as a dream to him. His ruling passion, now, is to find that lost shard of the runestone and to aid those Children made captive by forces uglier than any that have yet touched the Children of Ynell."

Canoldir picked up the starfires, placed them on the table before him, and began to arrange one next the other in the way they had been cut. Fitting perfectly, they made a rough oval but with a hole where one stone was missing. "The starfire that Telien carries." He then took up the two rune-stones. "Now tell the runestones for me, Ramad. Count them."

Ram pushed his bowl aside, gave Skeelie a long questioning look, then, unexpectedly, a comforting one. "The stone that I brought out of Tala-charen is lost in the sea, off the coast of Pelli."

"Yes."

"The stone that NilokEm brought out of Tala-charen and passed down to the dark twins is the stone in your left hand, given me by Hermeth.

Candoldir nodded.

"The stone in your right hand, the wraith dug out from beneath the mountain Tala-charen."

"Yes. You took it from the wraith at the moment that it possessed Telien."

Ram studied Canoldir. Did this man care that Telien had been taken by the wraith, that her very soul was captive? But why should he care? What was Telien to him?

"Continue, Ramad. What I care about is not of moment here. I would not have brought you here had I not intended to help you pursue Telien. Though I care for more than that. I care for the fate of the stones. And I care for a coupling you do not dream of; and of which I will know a long sorrow."

Ram watched him, unable to make sense of his words. "What coupling? What do you speak of in such riddles?" Yet the sense Skeelie caught from Canoldir's thoughts was so disturbing she upset her mug, occupied herself for some time mopping it up with her napkin.

Canoldir said softly, "Continue, Ramad, with the naming of the stones."

"The—the stone that Telien brought from out Tala-charen when she was first flung into Time, that stone is lost somewhere in darkness and she could not remember where. 'Lost in darkness. Found by the light of one candle, carried in a searching, and lost in terror,'" Ram repeated.

"That prediction, Ramad, is one of the wonders that moves through Time unchanged. Ever, ever changing are the winds of Time, ever nebulous and moving. And yet moments among those winds, words or predictions sometimes, the fate of a man sometimes, can move through those winds unchanging even as the swirling storms of Time change. 'Found again in wonder,' the prediction says. 'Given twice, and accompanying a quest and a conquering.' That is four stones, Ramad. What of the other five?"

"The fifth is the starfires, of course."

"Yes. Though the starfires do not hold the same magic as do the other runestones. The starfires know only their own magic, they know only the work of the core, which they are; they know only the magic to plunge into the core of Time." Canoldir lifted the ale pot from beside the hearth and poured out more of the spiced liquor into their empty mugs. "Five stones, then. Five you have accounted for. And what of the other four?"

"I do not know. I know only that all the shards must be brought together, that Ere cannot know peace until the runestone is whole once more. Four missing shards. Four—"

"No, Ramad. There are not four. There are only three."

"But I—"

"You carry the sixth runestone close to you. Do you not know what you carry?"

Ram stared at Canoldir. "I carry no other stone. I know no other stone. I carry no stone but these. What do you . . .?"

"Reach into your tunic, Ramad, and put on the table what you carry there."

Ram drew out from the folds of his tunic the only other object he carried and placed it on the table before Canoldir. The bitch wolf grinned in the firelight, her long rearing body turned red-gold before the flame. Ram raised his eyes to Canoldir, unbelieving.

Canoldir did not speak. The room began to fade, fog to come around them, then the space to warp and remake itself, so Ram and Skeelie stood in a small stone chamber lit with torches round the walls. A young man dressed in a deep blue robe knelt there in some private ritual; then suddenly a brilliant white light shattered around them and they were in Tala-charen, Ram a child again holding the shattered runestone in his hand while all around him came figures out of Time to receive those shards in one flashing instant, and among them the man in the blue robe. Ram recognized his face from having seen it in a vision long before; it was NiMarn, a younger NiMarn than Ram had seen, who had fashioned the bell of bronze. NiMarn, founder of the cult of the wolf. Time warped again, a dark-clad forgeman labored by NiMarn's side. The blaze of the forge flared and died and flared. He poured his molten metal, and NiMarn, in a strange, quick ceremony, placed the jade shard within. They saw the casting harden. They saw NiMarn raise the bronze bitch wolf aloft, smiling cruelly.

Long after the vision faded, Ram sat staring at Canoldir. When he spoke, his voice was barely audible. "How can it be? The wolf bell was already made when—when the runestone shattered. How...? It cannot be. The bell..."

"The turning in on itself of Time can be, Ramad. Not often does it happen, not even with the strongest powers. But the power that night on Tala-charen was power gone wild, power warping into new patterns, into new paths. Such a thing might never happen again, in all of Time. It was, it is. The jade is there inside the wolf bell and will remain so now until you yourself release it. Or until one close to you does. The sixth runestone of Eresu, hidden there inside the belly of the bitch wolf.

Ram touched the bronze wolf reverently. No wonder the bell had such power. And now—he lifted his eyes to Canoldir. "Three stones unaccounted for, then. Three stones to search out..." His voice caught with wonder.

"Three. But remember, Ramad, the wraith covets all of this," Canoldir said, sweeping up the two jade stones and the starfires into the leather pouch and tossing it to Ram.

ONCE, LATE IN THE NIGHT, Skeelie woke to hear the wolves howling on the mountain. She turned over, hardly aware of them, her thoughts all of Canoldir. Fawdref's voice raised in a wild, gleeful song, wailing, cleaving the night with furious joy. The others, the bitch and dog wolves, cleaved their voices to his in octaves like wild bugles ringing, crying out across the night against all that would fetter them.

Did another voice, a human voice, rise with their song, deep and abiding? Later, Skeelie could not be sure. She slept smiling, strangely unsettled.

151

# Chapter Ten

Skeelie woke at dawn. Somewhere, Canoldir was singing in a deep, wild voice that stirred a memory she could not bring clear; as if she had slept all night hearing his song, as if she had dreamed of him. Puzzling, she rose and began to dress; then she remembered suddenly, stopped half dressed to stare into space, seeing the hall last night, seeing Canoldir's face shadowed by firelight, hearing again his words.

Ram had left the hall, yawning. She had turned to leave when Canoldir stopped her with a look, and she had stood, her back to the dying fire, watching him.

"I cannot tell you what will happen, Skeelie, when you and Ramad follow the wraith. I can only tell you that I will put you where the wraith wanders. After that, there is nothing I can do. But I will tell you this. If you succeed in bringing Telien back with you, if you and Ramad succeed in rescuing her from the wraith and do not—are not destroyed yourselves, then—then, Skeelie of Carriol, I would speak with you." He had turned then, paced the length of the hall, turned again in shadow to pause, a bear of a man, his force filling the room. Then he returned to stand looking down at her. "If Ramad brings Telien away from the wraith, they will be—you will be wanting to be away from them."

Skeelie had stared into his eyes and nodded, her misery catching at her throat.

"If you will come to this place, Skeelie of Carriol, I would . . ." His dark eyes had looked so deep into hers she shivered. "I would court you!" he cried with a great shout. "I would court you! That is what I would do!" He had swung her around in a great dancing step like a bear, leaned to kiss her fiercely on the forehead, then had grown quiet, had led her down the corridor to her chamber, left her there with reluctance; she had felt his emotion like a tide, long after he had gone.

She stood clutching the door, filled with consternation. What was she to say to Canoldir this morning? That she would return if...? That she would not return? Yet she knew no answer was needed. No word need be spoken to Canoldir this morning—or ever, if she chose.

She thought of him with gladness, thought of his words with pleasure and with renewed strength. She stood day-dreaming for some time, then took up her sword and bow at last and left the chamber to find Ram.

She never reached the hall. Darkness swept around her; she was whirling in darkness. Canoldir's voice was singing deep but far away, his song ringing wildly. And Ram was there; they were tumbled on Canoldir's song. Time and song were one. They fell, were swept through voids of Time into rising light, into golden morning light, bouyed by Canoldir's song. Light burst through Time and through space as if they rode on liquid rays of sun. Ram shouted, but she could not make out the words. Canoldir's song rang with joy; Time itself leaped in his singing as they touched moments in their lives all but forgotten, drowned in sudden emotions as Canoldir's changing moods drowned them. His spirit surged; they could see his face sometimes as his shouting song rang down the wind; and the wolves came round them crying out in eerie mourning to join the song that leaped in cadences woven of all life.

Then Canoldir's voice faded. Was a whisper. Was gone.

They fell, terror-ridden, into darkness, their loss painful, cold gripping them. Down and down in darkness...

They stood in a cave made all of ice, ice walls gleaming, the wolves close around them taut with power and wonder, their eyes filled with predatory fire. Skeelie knelt and hugged Torc to her. How far had they come, how many years? In what time were they, and where? She lay her cheek against Torc's rough coat, hugged Torc hard, and the bitch wolf turned to lick her face. *You are choking the breath out of me, sister.*

Ram seemed confused. He stared at Skeelie for a long moment, hardly seeing her. Beyond the cave's ice walls was a pale, milky sky. Ere's two moons were thin crescents, white and lifeless. Skeelie approached the entrance, stood staring down appalled, then drew back. There was nothing there, nothing. No land below, only endless space. She shivered and pushed close to the others, chastened and afraid.

Ram made an effort to right his senses, felt for his sword, gave her a confused look that turned to defiance. Then at last he grinned, seemed himself again. "Great fires of Urdd, Skeelie, what kind of trip was that? Canoldir—great flaming thunder, what is he?"

"The man out of Time, Ramad. The man you went seeking."

"Like a whirlwind. I feel—I feel as if I've been trampled. Did *he* do all that, twist us, belt us through Time like that. Send us reeling down into this wretched place? It was never like that before. Not with all that thundering madness.

"And Skeelie—the wraith has been in this place, has traveled here."

"Yes." She could sense it, too. Sense that it was down there deep now, through the mountain, back through that narrow ice tunnel somewhere. She did not like to think about going in there. She felt in her tunic for flint, realized only then that she had no pack, no lantern, no mountain meat or blanket. She stared reproachfully at the leather pack slung securely across Ram's back. "Lantern, Ram? Food? I've nothing. Only my weapons."

"Why don't you have your pack? You were dressed. You—"

"I hadn't time. He swept me up—I'd hardly dressed!" She did not say she'd been daydreaming. "I'd left my pack in the hall."

"Yes, all right." He swung a lantern from out his pack,

sloshed the oil to see its level in the dim light, wondered that it had not all spilled away into unfathomable Time somewhere. He struck flint. The light caught and steadied. He held the lantern up. They stared. Skeelie shivered. It was not a cave to thrill them. All jagged ice, low. Cold went to the bone. Ram turned back to the cave mouth and stood looking, then returned. "No other way but this, then." They began to follow Fawdref, who had started ahead. Skeelie and Ram had to crouch almost at once beneath the low ceiling. The lantern light reflected wildly. The ice ceiling was cold against their backs. Soon they were cramped with the hunching, then reduced to crawling, then to wriggling on their bellies, Ram pushing his pack and the lantern ahead of him, Skeelie pushing the bows, trying not to panic. Ice burned their faces and fell inside their collars. At last they could stand again—at the lip of an icy cavern that cut deep into the earth below them.

Ice steps led down. Ram chopped at them with the tip of an arrow until they were rough enough to walk on. It was a long, steep descent, and when they reached the floor at last, they were dizzy with the glinting movement of lantern light across ice. The wolves stared into the depths of the cave, growling softly. *There is something there, Ramad.* Fawdref moved ahead slowly. *Something—though I cannot smell it. Something besides the wraith.* The sense of the wraith led them ahead in spite of the danger, following blindly the trail it had left between ice pillars. Soon the wolves began to move away from Ram and Skeelie, to disappear among the towers of ice until the two were alone. They went on alone for some time uneasily. Then Ram stopped, set the lantern down. But now, though the lantern was still, light continued to move around them, flashing and scurrying against the ice. They stood staring, weapons drawn, could see nothing but light moving as if light stalked them. As they started on again, light slipped across jutting ice ahead of them, then was still. High on their left, the ice seemed to move. On their right, a slithering motion caught in light. Where were the wolves? Not one was in sight. Their arrows were taut in their bows, but perhaps useless, for how can you kill light?

Then ahead of them a pale mass of light slithered, then turned and took shape. A giant white lizard, its scaly body nearly invisible against the white ice, its pale eyes on them, unseeing. They watched it for some moments.

"It is blind," Ram said at last. "Maybe it's harmless."

"Then why is it stalking us?" Skeelie kept her arrow taut. "I don't think it's so harmless."

They could see others now. Once their eyes grew accustomed, knew what to look for among the glancing ice, they could see three, four, then at last several dozen of the white creatures surrounding them, their blind faces turned toward them, their tongues curling in and out as if they could sense them by taste. Ram moved on. Skeelie followed. The lizards moved with them. There was no sign or sense of the wolves.

The attack came suddenly, a sound like breaking glass, an immense white shape flailing down at them across cracking ice. Ram sent an arrow into its soft belly as the creature twisted. Skeelie followed. One arrow, two. Then the wolves struck all at once. The creature screamed, blood flowed red against ice. It screamed again and sought them with blind eyes and reaching claws.

The wolves finished it quickly. It lay dying. The other lizards drew back, knowing danger in spite of their blindness, slithering away against pillars of ice. Ram and Skeelie pushed on, shivering with cold, the wolves close around them now. Suddenly Ram stopped, and pointed. "There. An opening. There is fire there! Look!"

She could see it then, a small cave opening far ahead through which fire glowed. She saw a flash of flame leap then die, then leap again. They started toward it, eager for warmth.

As they neared the fiery cave, the ice underfoot grew soft and they began to slosh through rivulets of water run-

ning down to puddle at their feet. Soon enough their boots
were soaked. They moved eagerly toward the warming
flame, watching it leap and die, stood at last in the entrance,
warming themselves. Soon their leathers grew so warm they
began to steam, though Skeelie could not get her feet warm
inside her soaking boots.

The cave of fire was not large, and the fire they must
skirt licked out to touch the walls. The heat grew so intense
they began to sweat beneath their steaming leathers. They
pushed ahead, but soon drew back again, nearly wild with
the heat. They stood again in the archway between the two
caves, heat pushing at their faces, the cold air from the cave
behind swirling up in welcome draft. Ram opened his collar,
shed his tunic. "We'll try it again, running. Make for that
opening at the far side."

But fire flared in their faces; there was the smell of
burning fur, and once more they pulled back, stood in the
ice cave, several wolves rolling in water to stifle the smol-
dering. A hank of Ram's hair was burnt.

"If we could stick ice to ourselves . . ." Skeelie offered.
"Water would make it stick to fur, maybe to leathers."

"The lizard skin would hold it, help protect us, it was
thick enough."

They returned to find a dozen lizards eating of the flesh
of their dead mate. The creatures had not touched the tough,
scaly skin, so Ram and Skeelie drove them off and began
to skin the creature. They cut the hide into large squares,
then began to break off slabs of ice from the pillars and
walls. As each wolf wet his coat in the runlets of melting
ice, Ram stuck ice slabs to him, and tied on a lizard skin.
When at last Ram and Skeelie were armored the same, they
entered the cave of fire and passed the flame, this time with
ease, stood at last in its far opening. There the night sky
shone with stars. The twin moons hung thin as scythes above
jagged peaks. They pulled off the skins and scraped off the
ice as best they could. A meadow rolled away down to a
moonlit valley and low hills. The wolves shook free of the

last of the ice and flung themselves out onto the meadow, rolling, drying themselves, giddy at being free of the mountain. Soon the smell of crushed grass filled the air. Ahead, beyond the hills, rose a diffused light as if houses stood there, with lamps burning.

They crossed three hills, and at last could see below them a large cluster of strange, cone-shaped dwellings. It appeared to be a city of rough earthen cones that might have been formed during some peculiar action of the volcanoes. Holes had been cut in the cones' sides for doors and windows, and through these, pale lamplight came. The sense of the wraith was strong, and a sense of defeat or hopelessness permeated the city.

"It is there, Skeelie. The wraith is in that place."

She could not answer, was cold with foreboding.

"We could wait for dawn," Ram said, watching her.

"We hadn't better. We'll be seen less at night."

"If you don't want to go, you needn't, you know."

"I want to go," she said quietly. He looked at her a long time and didn't say any more, started on.

The cobbled streets were so narrow between the rough stone cones that Ram and Skeelie, walking side by side, felt themselves forced together. The wolves pushed along the silent streets crowding them, wanting to stay close. Here and there a face looked out, silent and shadowed, or a figure stood unmoving in a lighted doorway. There was no sense of threat, but little sense of awareness, either.

Then a figure stepped out before them into the center of the street and shuffled toward them, a sour vacancy about it. Skeelie's hand trembled on her sword. But the being was only mindless and disgusting. Ram touched its dim instincts, twisted them, and made it turn back into the doorway. It stood there shuffling. It had been a man once, but was now a creature stripped of mind and soul. Nothing else approached them. They began to look inside the doors, where greasy lamps burned low. A grainery, long empty. A cobbler's hovel with only a few scraps of leather scattered in the dust. A dozen shops, all gone to decay, but with inner steps, not so dusty, leading up to sleeping rooms. And in some of the shops idle men stared back at them. A sweet, sticky smell pervaded the place. Ram soothed each creature they encountered, turned its mind away from them. "The wraith has made a city of slaves. It must feed on them, take their souls, then leave them alive to do the work of the city."

"Doesn't look like they do much work. And when it runs out of men to feed on, what then?" She turned to look at him suddenly, realizing only then the full implication of the strangeness of this land. "We are—we are in the unknown lands, Ram. Are there men in the unknown lands, then? Or did the wraith bring these people here?"

"I think—look at them, Skeelie. Touch the sense of them. I think these people are not of our countries, that they *are* people of the unknown lands. I think the wraith came here to them, that it took their city, simply moved in and did with them as it pleased. People we never knew about. Perhaps they did not know how to battle it, were not used to fighting, or to those who can touch their minds, Simple men."

"Why would it come here, so far? We don't know how far. If it wants the runestones?"

"It knew I would follow Telien, no matter how far. Maybe—it wanted people, many people perhaps, to put under its power and draw strength from. Once it learned to take the strength from a person, I suppose its power has increased quickly."

"And we go to challenge it." She studied him, trying to look certain of their own strengths. Feeling shaky.

They stood at last before the cone that formed the central tower, a lopsided volcanic cone laid down by fire and silt and ash, then carved by water and wind into its thick coned shape. It had been hollowed out by men long before the wraith came. They saw a balcony high up and narrow. Did a shadow move inside? They could not be sure. The sense of the wraith was now so strong Skeelie felt sick with it: the sense of its desire to conquer them; of its greed for the runestones. Yet also a sense of its fear. Perhaps, even now, it did not feel certain of its power over this angry band armed with the shards of the runestone. Torc stood with flattened ears, her lips pulled back, her hatred risen to fury. The wolves flanked her, sharing her hatred, their heads lowered and fangs bared, watching the entrance to the tower. Skeelie laid her hand on Torc's shoulder, but did not pull the wolf to her; there was too much anger there, too much hatred. *You must not kill it, Torc.*

Torc turned, snarling at her. *I know that, sister. I know we must release Telien. But then, once Telien is free, then I can kill the wraith. Once you and Ramad are away.*

Skeelie's fear for Torc was painful. Torc ignored it, had no fear for herself, no thought for herself save revenge.

Ram had left them, gone back into a narrow street, entered a doorway. Skeelie, watching the empty street, could not sense what he was about. He emerged at last, propelling one of the mindless men before him, a big brute of a fellow who must once have been formidable indeed. She could touch no sense of what Ram was about. Why did he block her from his thoughts? Did he plan to force the wraith to take that man's body, to leave Telien and enter that body? It was strong enough, surely. But how make the wraith do such a thing? It would rather have Ram, a Seer. Rather have her own Seer's skills to add to its own. Did Ram think that with the power of the runestones he could force the wraith to abandon Telien?

She could feel his concentration, his single-minded commitment, but she could not read his intention. Did he, she wondered, growing cold, mean to make a trade? Give the wraith this hostage in return for Telien, but with some bribe it could not resist?

What bribe? What bribe except—her hands shook. She stared at Ram.

Did he mean to use the one bribe the wraith could never

resist? Use the runestones? Trade the runestones of Eresu, trade all of Ere then, for the life of Telien? Oh, but he would not.

She followed Ram, cold and silent inside herself, watching him and unable to sense anything from his closed, remote state as he forced the hostage toward the wraith's door. He did not pound on the heavy planks, but simply lifted the latch and forced the door in, pushing the captive ahead of him.

But the way was blocked by a little square woman no taller than Ram's waist. She stared up at them with a face as sour as spoiled mash. "Go away. The goddess does not see strangers." Her coarse brown skirt and apron were none too clean, and her hair seemed not to know what a comb was. She looked them up and down, looked disgusted at the crowding wolves, then began to push against the door in an effort to close it. Ram held it back with a light touch, watched her with amusement. She glowered. "Go away, I said! The goddess sees no one! She does not want strangers here."

"She will see us," Ram said. "The goddess will see us." He stepped forward, propelling the prisoner, but the little woman held her ground. Behind her, in a dim sunken room, dozens of servants were working at an odd assortment of tasks, all crowded together among tables and benches and baskets with little order, seeming to be always in each other's way. Their talk had died, but now began to rise again.

"The goddess Telien will see us," Ram repeated, and had the satisfaction of seeing the woman's startled look, at the mention of Telien's name. "If she does not see us, we will turn her magic to ashes, and you as well, old woman." He pointed a finger at her nose. "If we do not see the goddess, *you* will be swept like dust, old woman, in the winds I will call forth to destroy your goddess!"

The little woman scurried away so fast that both Ram and Skeelie grinned. They watched her run almost agilely up a narrow stair carved into the stone wall. Then they stood looking down with curiosity upon the seething activity in the workroom, where folk scraped vegetables, mended furniture, butchered a sheep, kneaded bread, all side by side in a confused huddle. It seemed that all the tasks of this rough castle were performed in this one room—and performed mostly at night. Was night the natural time of waking, here in this land? The smells of paint and fresh-sawed wood and warm blood mixed with the smell of baking bread. On the rough walls, one could see pick marks where the soft stone had been carved away. But the walls were carved with other things, too, with the images of figures.

"Let's have a look," Ram said, and led her down the few steps to the main room. The wolves remained behind guarding the hunched, still figure that once had been a man.

There were goddesses carved into the walls. Tall, beautiful women carved into the stone; but with the taint of evil about them. Farther back in the room they ceased to be beautiful and became goddesses of lust in poses that made Skeelie blush. And in the shadows at the back of the room, there were goddesses sacrificing tortured men in savage ceremonies. Skeelie and Ram avoided looking at each other. Around them, the servants worked unheeding. Skeelie could smell rotting vegetables, rancid oil. They stepped over tools left lying where they had been dropped. As they circled the room, the carved images grew so disturbing that Skeelie wanted to turn away from them, yet could not turn away from their twisted ugliness. And each depraved image had the face of Telien.

Ram turned away at last, ashen. Skeelie could do nothing to comfort him, nothing to soften the ugliness.

The stumpy woman returned and, without speaking, led them across the littered floor, through sawdust and food trimmings, to the stair and up it. A narrow, steep stair unprotected by any railing. Skeelie felt she was climbing the side of the wall like a fly. The wolves came behind, pushing the prisoner along between them. The sense of the wraith there above, the sense of impending danger increased as the little band climbed up the side of the cavernous room. Skeelie wanted to turn and pelt down the stairs, did not want to face what could happen here. She shielded her thoughts from Ram, or hoped she was shielding them, forcing herself to climb, staring above her at Ram's rigid leather-clad back.

# Chapter Eleven

THE STAIR ROSE DIRECTLY into a large, rough room cluttered with garish furnishing: purple satin drapings; magenta bedcover encrusted with tarnished gold braid; black and lavender pillows; all of it soiled and worn; and covered with a heavy smell, sweet and disgusting. They did not see Telien at first.

When Ram saw her, standing still in the shadow by the hearth, he caught his breath and was with her at once, forgetting caution. He touched her arm, awash with the shock of seeing the parody she had become. Her soiled silk frock was pulled tight, so low her pale, tangled hair fell over half-concealed breasts. Wide bracelets covered her arms nearly to the elbow; her feet were bare, with toe rings and anklets; her face was painted with a hard flush over her palor; her green eyes were dull and deeply shadowed, her face gaunt. She stood so still she might indeed have been one of the carved figures. Skeelie could feel Ram's sick mourning, watched him reach out to hold Telien in spite of his horror. Only then did Telien move, to pull away from him.

Ram stepped back, but reached out in spirit to her trapped soul as if he sought an injured, frightened bird inside a dark, puzzling trap. His emotions were subdued, cool now and apprizing of Telien, touching then drawing back, reaching again, trying to awaken Telien, to make her fight from within.

The wraith watched him. It did not move or change expression, though its skin seemed to grow more sallow beneath the painted rouge. Telien's green eyes, flat with the death-spirit, observed Ram and delved deep within Ram seeking weakness or fear.

Then suddenly it brought a power down upon Ram so

violent he stumbled, then steadied himself against the side of a chair. Skeelie threw all her force against the wraith's dark spirit. *The stones, Ram! Use the stones!* He seemed frozen, unable to think. She could feel the wolves' force joining with hers. At last Ram reached into his tunic slowly, as if in a dream, and clutched the leather pouch in his fist. The wraith stared, lusting for those stones, then drew back as Ram righted his senses, as the power of Ram and wolves and Skeelie joined with the stones to rise to a crescendo that trembled the room. Fury flashed from the wraith's eyes. And then Ram began to part the intricate shields with which the wraith guarded itself, so that for a brief moment Telien was there, soft and terrified and begging Ram for help.

But the wraith rallied, Telien was gone, the green eyes cold with hate.

Now Ram knew that Telien lived, he wanted to tear the wraith from her. He forgot everything in his black fury as his hands gripped its throat. He was intent only on releasing Telien. The wraith cowered, shrank down in pain beneath his clutching fingers—but it was Telien's pain, too. "Don't kill her, Ram!" Skeelie's voice shattered him, shocked him. He stared at his hands on Telien's throat and let her go. She slumped. He caught her and held her to him, could feel her heart pounding; could feel the wraith's desperate rise of strength as it began to suspect that perhaps Ram could destroy it. It began to falter beneath the power of the several stones, beneath the power of this crew joined. They stood locked in a maze of powers while above the town the stars wheeled toward the horizon and the moons swam slowly down behind black peaks. A tableau of powers, motionless, Ram and Skeelie facing the painted parody of Telien, the wolves frozen into positions of attack, the mindless captive Ram had brought from the town huddled against the door. The moons set and a pale hint of dawn touched the night sky, and neither force gave quarter. Telien came forth sometimes, battling; but then weakening with the powers pulling at her. She would sink then, so the wraith emerged stronger in its desperation. Then the wraith began to reach into the room, to awaken the captive. The big man stirred and straightened and seemed to clutch at consciousness. Fawdref spun, snarling. The wolves moved as one. The captive struck out at them, and lunged. But there were too many wolves, they brought the man down at Skeelie's feet. "Don't kill it, Fawdref," she whispered, and Ram echoed her.

"Don't kill it! Drive it here to me."

The wolves forced the injured man to crawl the length of the room. Skeelie watched, strung taut with fear. The formless shadow of the wraith must be released from Telien. Ram turned on the wraith with a fury yet unmatched, jerked it by the arm ignoring Telien's pain. He was concerned now only with Telien's life. He jerked her to him, stared down at her, then shoved her toward the prisoner, which cowered bleeding before the wolves. "Enter it," he breathed to the wraith. "Enter the man you have destroyed. Finish what you began!" And when the wraith refused, Ram forced it against the wall, did not let himself think that if he hit it, he would be hitting Telien. Its parody of Telien stared back at him, hating him. "Make the captive stand up again, creature of shadows. Make it stand, and enter it!"

The painted face of Telien stared coldly back at him. But fear showed deep in its eyes. "Make it stand!" Ram repeated.

At last the creeping prisoner at Ram's feet stood up slowly and stared at Ram, uncomprehending.

"Enter it," Ram said. "Enter it, creature of dark. Or I will destroy both you and the girl, never doubt it." His power was like nothing Skeelie had seen. She watched Ram bring the power of the stones around the wraith in a roaring burst of air that so nearly shattered their ears that a wolf cried out in pain and a wind tore at the room.

"Enter it or I will destroy your soul. Snuff you like a candle!"

The wraith cringed before him; Telien's thin body shivering in the black gown. Dark fear welled in its eyes, and two images vied for reflection in that painted face, as in a deep-seeing mirror; the wraith's cruel presence and the image of Telien.

"Enter the captive and leave Telien. Become this man, or I will crush your soul for you."

Skeelie watched Ram and knew he had no idea whether he could destroy the wraith's soul, though his power tore at the very fiber of the wraith's being. The wraith cringed again, stared at Ram uncertainly, drew its spirit back, pressed its hands to its face in fear and confusion—to Telien's face. It was Telien there.

Telien, alone. Telien, filled with sickness, slumping against Ram. And the tall, powerful captive rose and stared at Ram, its eyes the wraith's dead eyes. It reached for Ram. He pushed Telien away from him and drew his sword in one swift motion, battled the creature knowing he dare not kill it and release the wraith again. As the wraith's darkness touched his mind, he felt himself begin to weaken. He fought in desperation, driving the creature back until it plunged across a cushioned bench and fell; but it sprang up again, broke the leg off the bench as if it were kindling, and came at Ram. The wolves stood tensed, ready to spring.

Skeelie held Telien close to her, for the girl was so weak she could not stand alone. She was so very thin, her skin cold and damp. Skeelie smoothed her hair, talked softly to her as one would to a frightened child. She was so diminished it seemed that the sickness of the wraith had invaded her very blood. They watched the battle with growing fear. Then Ram slashed the bench leg from the wraith's hand and began backing it against the bed. He struck and wounded it with a long sword slash down chest and belly, so it doubled up and fell.

"Don't kill it, Ram! You..."

But Ram was backing away. Skeelie saw Torc surge past to stand over it, wanting to kill.

"Don't, Torc! It would take Ram!"

Torc snarled deep in her throat, her bared teeth inches from the man's face. *When you are gone, sister, I will kill*

167

*it. Go—get Ramad and Telien from this place, get away
from here. This creature will die, and you must be away.*

*It could take you, Torc. Become you.*

*It cannot, sister. Such as this cannot enter into the soul
of the wolf.*

*Are you so sure?*

Torc did not answer, turned her mind to Ram, spoke her
silent words to him. *You will go away, Ramad. Send them
all away, the people, the servants, so that I can be alone
with this creature.*

Ram hardly heard her; he had taken Telien from Skeelie
and now held her close. Telien clung to him weeping, her
hands gripping his arm as if she were afraid he would disappear, or that she would again be torn from him. Skeelie
was filled with pain, with empathy for them both. The
broken man that was now the wraith lay unconscious, bleeding badly. Skeelie stared at it, knew if it awoke it could yet
possess Ram.

*Get them out of here, sister. Turn the servants out, get
Ramad and Telien from this place.*

Skeelie knelt to hug Torc, then left her, grabbed Ram's
arm and began to pull him and Telien toward the stair.

*When you are gone from this place, when everyone is
away, I will kill it. Or I will wait for it to die from the
wounds of Ramad's sword and from thirst. I will not leave
this place, sister, until the soul of the wraith, with no other
body to enter, fades and dies. It is weakened now from
battle, it must have a body near, or it will fade—to nothing,
sister! To nothing!*

BY THE TIME DAWN lit the city of cones, the wraith's hall
was vacant. The simple folk were streaming obediently
away, out through the city to take refuge in the surrounding
hills until they could return to their homes. Already the
domination of the wraith had begun to lift, and it seemed
to Ram and Skeelie that the folk would return to their own
natures unharmed.

Ram carried Telien. They left the folk of the city of cones at the foothills and began to climb the first ridge, rocky and steep. Telien weighed no more than a child. There were no trails in this wild land. They ascended jagged rock shoulders until they stood at last high above the wraith's city on the crest of a range that looked not over the countries they knew, but over land completely unknown to any of their own peoples. They were tired nearly beyond bearing, and once over the mountain's high ridge and a bit down the northwest side, they found a sheltered grassy place tucked between boulders where they could sleep. They rested until the noon sun, lifting over the ridge, woke them.

They took a light meal of mawzee cakes and mountain meat, though Telien ate only a few bites. She was very weak and pale, shivering even in the warm cloak Ram had found for her in the wraith's hall and she remained silent. It was as if the effort to speak, or even to gather her thoughts, was too great. They started down the mountain at last, Ram tense with worry over Telien, carrying her most of the way. Below them lay a deep valley, green and dotted with lakes and spanned down its length by a river. The scent of green came up to them, a scent of wildness that made the wolves raise their faces to the wind, then go melting off down the mountain far ahead of them, heads up, seeking out over the new land. There were trees here none of them had ever seen, unfamiliar plants. They had no idea how far into the unknown lands they had been cast.

They reached the valley at dusk, Telien asleep against Ram's shoulder. There was no sign of people, and the returning wolves brought no word of any. *The land is empty, Ramad,* Fawdref told him quietly. *Empty as far as we ranged.* The wolves had come streaming back drunk with new scents and bringing game such as Ram and Skeelie had never seen: a small red deer no bigger than the wolves themselves; a fat fowl larger than a chidrack, gray and long-necked, with a crest to its head like a great fan.

They found an outcropping of granite that formed a shallow cave. Ram laid Telien inside and covered her with his blanket, then built a fire. Skeelie thought with longing of the blankets and food they had in their haste left behind in the cone tower, snatching up only the cloak for Telien; then thought of Torc alone there and went silent with worry. Rhymannie came to press against her, knowing her fears; knowing Skeelie could not understand why none of the wolves had remained with Torc, why they had left her so very alone. *As she wanted to be,* Rhymannie said. *As any of us would want. It is different with wolves, perhaps. Alone with the thing you have to do. Or perhaps not so different. But, sister, Torc will come to us in her own time.*

"If she comes at all," Skeelie said, turning her face away. She rose and went out of the cave to stand on a little rise, looking out at the darkening valley.

When she returned to the shelter, Telien lay with her face turned to the inner wall of overhanging rock, her breathing shallow and fast, her skin clammy. Ram knelt beside her holding the waterskin, but Telien refused to drink. The pain on Ram's face was terrible. Skeelie knew that even had she herbs she was not sure what she might have attempted to use, so alien was Telien's sickness. When Telien opened her eyes at last, to stare up at Ram, she did not know him. He took her hand, but she drew away, wincing. Gently, Ram began to feel into her mind. Skeelie followed and was shocked at her sinking, empty weakness, at the feeling inside Telien as if she were falling down into blackness and could not stop. "Where is Ram?" Telien whispered. "Ram has not left me?"

"I am here, Telien. I am holding you."

Telien stared up at him, her green eyes dull with the inner sickness, with the knowledge that rode within her of her own wasting.

Ram slept close to Telien that night, warming her, the wolves all around warming her as well, for she complained of cold that cut deep into her bones. Skeelie lay stretched out at the edge of the shelter as far from Ram and Telien as she could manage, so painful was it to see the two of them torn apart, to see Ram hurting, and she unable to help either of them. She tried to give Telien strength with her own powers, but the sinking, falling sensation that gripped Telien all but defeated her. If she gave Telien anything at all, she feared it was not enough.

Dawn came sharp with a cool wind. Skeelie sat up and looked back into the cave where all lay still asleep. We will go on this morning, she thought. The three of us and the wolves. Then when Telien is better, I will turn back, find my way back—home. Home? And where is that?

Where would home be now, for her? Now that Ram had Telien?

A place out of Time, perhaps. A place with Canoldir, if he still wanted her.

She turned to look back into the shelter, feeling uneasy suddenly, feeling something very out of place. Ram and Telien lay as before, close but not touching, Ram's arm thrown over his face as he was wont to sleep when he was exhausted or very worried. As she watched, the wolves stirred, and Fawdref rose suddenly to look across at her, his golden eyes dark with grief. She saw Ram wake from sleep and pull Telien closer, looking down at her. Saw him go pale, touch Telien's cheek. Then he pressed his face into Telien's lifeless shoulder, and clutched her to him so her arm dragged limp across the blanket.

He remained that way until the sun came bright. He might have remained that way much longer, wanting to die there with her, had not Fawdref nosed him up at last and made him rise and turn away from her. Ram's face was twisted and unnatural with his pain. Skeelie could not speak or look at him.

THEY BURIED HER high on an alpine meadow, in a grave that could look out over lands no man of Ere had ever seen. Ram would have buried the starfire with her, which they had found folded into her gown—for luck, for safe travel, or in some wild pagan notion that it might carry her back through Time and make her live again. But at Skeelie's look, he knew that he must take it. It was the core of the runestone; without it, though he might someday find and bring together all the other shards, the runestone would lie incomplete. *She will travel far without it, Ramad,* Fawdref told him. *She will know other lives.*

"How can you be sure! *Our* lives will never touch again!"

Yellow wolf eyes watched him. Unfathomable. *I cannot know if your lives will touch again, Ramad. Nor can you. I only know that she will live, perhaps in more joy even than this life gave her.*

"*More* joy? She had no joy. She had only pain. Fear of her father. The beatings. Then carried into Time. The wraith—"

*She had joy, Ramad. Joy in you.* Fawdref turned away then and went up into the hills, a dark, shaggy shadow melting among boulders, carrying darkness with him. It did not settle well with the great wolves to feel human pain so closely, pain of friend, unless that friend were bent on mending the pain. Just now, Ramad was not.

Skeelie stood at the base of the hill looking after Fawdref and knowing his thoughts: Ram must mend himself and no one could do that for him. She was surprised to find that his thoughts lifted her suddenly, made her feel lighter.

*Must* Ram mend himself, was the great wolf right? She felt a presence, then, in her mind, and looked up into the sun-bright wind; a craggy, lined face, a bear of a man, blackbearded; dark-eyes watched her in a vision so sharp it made her catch her breath. *What will you do, Skeelie of Carriol?*

*I will go with Ram.*

*And if he doesn't want you?*

*Only time will tell that.*

*I live with all of Time. I can wait, then.*

*You must not wait for me.*

*There will be others. A man does not well, always alone.*

*They will be transient ones. But if you come to me, Skeelie of Carriol, I will belong to you for all time. All Time will be yours to wander. If so you choose. Go with him now, and be happy. Even in his pain, make him happy. Beyond his pain, give him joy.*

The sun shone strong. The figure was gone, the thoughts gone. Ram stood at some distance, where boulders crowned the hill, had turned, was watching her. He said nothing, just looked. Perhaps, she thought, he could mourn Telien without destroying himself with the pain. He came to her at last, stood looking down at her, the sun making his hair like fire. "You would go with Canoldir if it were not for me."

"I mean to go with you."

They looked at each other a long time.

At last Ram shouldered his pack, cuffed Skeelie in a poor imitation of the old roughness between them, and looked up to where the wolves stood watching them. Then he started off southward, in the direction where home must be, for all the unknown lands lay to the north of the eleven countries of Ere. How far they were from the lands they knew, from a time that would have meaning for them, they had no idea. Skeelie felt Ram's despondency, his deep mourning for Telien. But there was something else, a deep abiding purpose that lay strong within him. She watched him take the white goatskin pouch from his tunic and touch the runestones briefly, then clutch the pouch tight in his hand. He quickened his pace, striking off toward the head of the valley. She hurried beside him, the warmth of the lifting sun on her cheek.

But she stopped suddenly, hardly in her stride, to stare up at the eastern mountains.

She felt the high howling before she heard it. Felt in her soul the wailing that, in another moment, would split the air over the mountain. The wolves stood alert, sensing that vibration, looking eastward up the mountain, holding within themselves the vibration of that far, silent wail.

Then they heard it, far and clear. A keening of cold, lonely victory. And they lifted their muzzles and cried out a reply that sent chills rippling the still mountain air.

She would come now. Torc would come.

SHIRLEY ROUSSEAU MURPHY grew up in California riding the horses her father trained. She attended the San Francisco Art Institute and has been a commercial artist and interior decorator designing everything from breadboxes to beaded wedding gowns. She has written many books for young readers and is currently living with her husband in Georgia.